JOCELYN

JOCELYN

John Galsworthy

Introduction by Catherine Dupré

DUCKWORTH/SIDGWICK & JACKSON
LONDON

*First published in this edition by Gerald Duckworth and Co. Limited and
Sidgwick and Jackson Limited in 1976.*

*Copyright © The John Galsworthy Estate
Introduction © 1976 Catherine Dupré*

*Originally published by Gerald Duckworth and Co. in
1898 under the pseudonym of John Sinjohn.*

ISBN 0 283 98244 6

*Printed in Great Britain
by The Anchor Press Ltd
and bound by Wm Brendon & Son Ltd
both of Tiptree, Essex*

Introduction

by Catherine Dupré

Jocelyn is the first full length novel of John Galsworthy; it is also the only novel that he completely rejected in later years, and refused ever to have reprinted. The first and only edition was published in 1898 under the pseudonym that Galsworthy used for his first four books, John Sinjohn, and of this edition only 750 copies were distributed in this country.

The year before, 1897, Galsworthy had published at his own expense a volume of short stories, *From the Four Winds*. This first publication was rightly relegated to oblivion; "that dreadful little book" its author wrote of it in the last year of his life. But *Jocelyn* deserves a better fate, and unlike its predecessor should now take its place among the works of John Galsworthy. Artistically it is an uneven book; excessively romantic, often melodramatic, it nevertheless contains some excellent pieces of writing, and a sense of comedy that was to become all too rare in Galsworthy's later work.

To appreciate fully *Jocelyn* it is essential to know something of the circumstances of Galsworthy's life at this period, for in common with many first novels *Jocelyn* is a very personal book, and its material is drawn almost entirely from the life of its author.

John Galsworthy was born in 1867. He was the son of a London solicitor whose family had recently become rich by extensive and prudent speculation in property in the rapidly developing City. His father's family had originated in Devon, and it was John's grandfather, also a John Galsworthy, who was the first member of it to settle in London. Blanche Bailey Bartleet, Galsworthy's mother, came of a family of superior social origins, a fact of which she was extremely conscious, and one which she was anxious to impress on her children; but despite this "superiority" Blanche Galsworthy was a silly and trivial woman, and it was from their father that the children inherited their exceptional intelligence, combined with artistic leanings. John was the elder son of the four children; Lilian was two years older than him, Hubert and Mabel both younger. His sister Lilian at first seemed the most talented and intellectual of the children, and it was almost certainly her influence, her stimulating conversation, her mind that ranged widely from philosophy to music and literature, that led her brother John to begin to question his parents' assumption that he should follow a professional career, probably that of the law.

To counteract this restlessness, John Galsworthy senior decided to send his elder son abroad, first to America, and then to New Zealand and the South Seas. It was on the latter journey that John met Joseph Conrad, then the first mate on the famous sailing ship, s.s. *Torrens*. Conrad was already working on his first novel *Almayer's Folly*, and on the long voyage from Adelaide to Cape Town the two men, who were both ultimately to become writers of distinction, spent long hours discussing their ideas and hopes. This marked the beginning of a friendship that was to last until Conrad's death in 1924. But for Galsworthy it had a deeper significance; this meeting with a man who was already committed to a life of writing had a decisive influence on him. It swayed the balance conclusively; he would at least attempt to become a writer. "I do wish I had the gift of writing, I really think that is the nicest way of making money going," he wrote wistfully to Monica Sanderson, the sister of Ted Sanderson with whom he had travelled to Australia.

It was while in this mood of uncertainty that Galsworthy became acquainted with his cousin Arthur Galsworthy's wife, Ada. Ada was already the intimate friend of John's sisters, and from them he learnt of the extreme unhappiness of Ada's marriage. John and Ada were immediately attracted to each other; they soon became close friends and in September 1895 they became lovers.

Ada Galsworthy was thirty-one years old when she and John began their illicit liaison, some three years older than John. Even before her marriage to Major Galsworthy her life had been an unhappy one; unfortunately the circumstances of her early life are difficult to establish, and she herself was unwilling that they should be made known. In John Galsworthy's first biography, written by H. V. Marrot and published only two years after his death, the only facts that she gives about herself are that she was born on 21 November 1866, and that she was the daughter of a Dr. Emanuel Cooper of Norwich. Both these facts are incorrect. From papers recently discovered, it appears that Ada was the *adopted* daughter of Emanuel Cooper, and that she was born two years earlier than the date given in Marrot's biography. (It seems probable that she falsified her birth date so that she might appear to be Dr. Cooper's daughter, rather than because of any wish to hide her age.) Her mother, Anna Julia Pearson, was almost certainly never Emanuel Cooper's wife, and it seems probable that her two children, Ada and Arthur, were illegitimate; certainly Ada was conceived in a spirit of hatred and despair, and when she was born her mother gave the wretched child the name Ada *Nemesis.* How Emanuel Cooper came to adopt Mrs. Pearson's children may never be known; one can only surmise that the elderly and eccentric doctor longed for heirs who would carry on the name of Cooper, that possibly, as an obstetrician, he came across the two unwanted children, and decided to "adopt" them. But adoption did not apparently mean giving the children a home or father in the ordinary sense of the word; Mrs. Pearson and her children were accommodated in an extremely modest dwelling in Norwich, the property of the doctor, and allowed only sufficient money for their support and education. In his will Dr. Cooper left Ada an independent woman of moderate means.

This then was the woman who became Galsworthy's mistress, an act of considerable courage in 1895. For ten years John and Ada accepted that this half-shared life was all that was available to them; a divorce between Ada and Major Galsworthy they both felt would be too distressing to John's father, especially if it were followed by the marriage of Ada to his son. It was only after John Galsworthy senior's death in 1904 that John and Ada lived openly together, thus forcing the Major to divorce his wife. In September 1905 John and Ada were legally married. But during these ten years Ada was much more than a mistress to John; it was her encouragement and determination that gave John the confidence he so much needed to enable him to write. Everything he wrote, even the short stories that made up the volume *From the Four Winds,* Ada praised and criticised; he might despair of his ability but she would not. She became, what she was to be for the whole of their lives together, his amanuensis.

Whether it was her idea or his that he should write the story of their romance one will never know, but this in fact is what John did, and *Jocelyn* is the first account of his love affair with Ada Galsworthy. It was a theme that Galsworthy was to return to again and again in the course of his writing life, the story of two lovers who are not free to marry because one of the partners is unhappily married to another person. The most famous, and by far the most successful, use of this theme was to be *The Man of Property,* the story of Irene and Soames Forsyte; but by the time this novel was published, in 1906, the Galsworthys were married and, despite the remonstrances of his family, neither Ada nor John minded if a parallel was seen between the fictional story and their own lives.

In 1898 concealment was still necessary, and it would seem likely that it was a poor attempt to disguise the similarity to their own situation that made Galsworthy cast Jocelyn, the heroine of the novel, as the free partner, and Giles Legard, who falls in love with her, the one who is tied by his marriage to Irma, an invalid.

A more fundamental difference between *Jocelyn* and its later prototypes is the attitude of the lovers: in this early novel the feelings of the characters are much more exposed; the frustrated passion of Giles Legard covers page after page, as too does the bitter remorse that Jocelyn feels when she has allowed herself to accept Giles' passionate advances. The lovers of Galsworthy's later novels have much less guilt about their illicit loving; they are also much more reticent about expressing their feelings, or allowing their author to do so for them. It is this lack of restraint, this openness of feeling, that makes *Jocelyn* so very different from Galsworthy's later novels; even the style of the writing is much freer, much less formal, than that of his more mature work. As he developed as a writer, at the height of his achievement, this severe control, both of style and of character, is very marked. *The Man of Property* is an extremely formal novel; it is about people whose lives are lived according to a strict pattern; even the love affair of Irene and Bosinney is like a *pas de deux* in a ballet, and at the only point when a character loses control, i.e. the probable suicide of Bosinney, the story becomes unconvincing.

Much of the interest of *Jocelyn* is that its heroine, Jocelyn Ley, is Galsworthy's portrait of Ada as he first knew her. Few readers will find Jocelyn's character a sympathetic one: one can see the attraction she had for Giles Legard, her vitality, her youthfulness, the sharp contrast to his invalid wife; but at the same time she appears as selfish and hard, too often coldly aloof to the appeals of her suffering lover. "He caught her suddenly in his arms, and held her face to his, kissing it passionately. The tears ran down his face and wetted her cheeks—her eyes were dry." This paragraph is typical of their relationship—and one suspects also of that of Ada and John Galsworthy.

Jocelyn as a fictional portrait of Ada has in it a blunt truth that is lacking in Galsworthy's later portraits: Irene Forsyte is a cold woman, but depicted as a very perfect one, so also is the fragile and over-sensitive Audrey Noel of *The Patrician* (incidentally Ada's favourite of her husband's novels). And yet *Jocelyn* was written when Galsworthy was most passionately and blindly in love, during the first years of their romantic association.

In judging Jocelyn, or Ada, one must always bear in mind the exceptionally unhappy circumstances of Ada's early life; Major Ley, Jocelyn's father, like Emanuel Cooper, died when Jocelyn was very young, leaving her in the care of his sister, Mrs. Travis, a woman "for whom he had a certain contemptuous affection. The two ladies, marvellously dissimilar, got on fairly well together—perhaps because they never remained for long at a time in one place, perhaps because neither expected to understand the other, nor required much at her hands." This is a fairly accurate description of Ada's relationship with her mother. Mrs. Cooper and Ada, like Mrs. Travis and Jocelyn, had spent four years in almost constant travelling, and Galsworthy says of Jocelyn, "From her mother, in whose family there was a tradition of gipsy blood, she had inherited a restless, moody nature, which ordained that she should wander . . .". This strange hint of "gipsy blood" may in fact be a clue to the identity of Ada's father—it seems such unlikely parentage for a girl born conventionally in wedlock, as Jocelyn was.

Ada's restlessness was in fact to prove the one respect in which she and John as partners were least compatible, and it is interesting to see that this passion for being forever on the move was already so much part of her character when she first met John. "Why aren't we in Paris?" Jocelyn complains to Mrs. Travis. "Chelsea's nice for London, but I'm so sick of London!" How often in later years Ada must have expressed almost exactly that feeling to John, or to her life-long friend and confidant, the writer R. H. Mottram. "Longings for a far-away holday are simply gnawing me . . ." she wrote to him. Similarly "Jocelyn hated the grey monotony of English skies. She had a fierce love of the sun . . .". So it was that each winter John and Ada Galsworthy left England for the Tyrol, the south of France, and in later years the United States, where Ada found the climate of California particularly congenial. John, especially as he grew older, would have been far happier to remain in England, in the lonely farmhouse, Wingstone, on the edge of Dartmoor, or later at Bury House on the Sussex downs.

How closely Jocelyn's aunt, Mrs. Travis, resembled Ada's mother one will never know; as a character in fiction she is delightful, but in real life she would have made a trying and boring companion. She is absurdly complacent and trivial in her outlook; her main obsession is a roulette "system" which she cannot understand, or use profitably, but in order to practise it she makes a daily pilgrimage to Monte Carlo accompanied by the unwilling Jocelyn. Her philosophy—if it can be called such—is one in which all things and people are seen entirely as they relate to her; thus when Giles Legard (who is a relation of hers) loses weight "she resented the dwindling of his bulk; . . . perhaps, in some mysterious way, she regarded it as the removal of her own property". She even has to hurry especially to catch trains because "she had always a conviction that trains wished to elude her". From this first novel one might have hoped that Galsworthy would develop this talent for comedy, in fact truly comic characters are very rare in the later novels, and when he deliberately sets out to write a humorous book such as *The Burning Spear* it is a complete disaster.

Why one must ask, did Galsworthy finally reject *Jocelyn*? As a first novel it has much that is good in it; as the first novel of a writer of international reputation it is a book of exceptional interest. Moreover Galsworthy allowed a mass of writing to be printed and reprinted that frankly should never have got further than his wastepaper basket; why then was *Jocelyn* along with *From the Four Winds* doomed to oblivion? The answer is almost certainly a personal one : *Jocelyn* is much too revealing. It expresses feelings and emotions that the older writer would never have put on paper; it shows a man suffering terribly from his frustrated passion for a woman. Later in life Galsworthy would have condemned such self-revelation. Moreover, reading it later and in a more dispassionate mood, it must have struck him that his portrait of Ada as Jocelyn Ley was not an entirely flattering one. He loved her, Giles Legard loved her, but would his readers love her? Would they not see her as an extremely hard and rather selfish young woman? "... you don't care how you hurt me," Giles exclaims to Jocelyn in agony, and "She pressed her lips tightly together. He could not help the swift thought, 'She is cruel', and hated himself for it in the same breath." Ada Galsworthy was a woman who had been badly hurt by life; she loved John Galsworthy as much as she was capable of loving, but she was nevertheless a cold, unpassionate woman. John loved Ada, but he suffered from her lack of warmth; he suffered too from her selfish need to travel. *Jocelyn* had an almost naïve truth that first novels sometimes have; but it was a truth that Galsworthy did not want the world to know.

The rejection of *Jocelyn* was more than the rejection of one novel. Had Galsworthy pursued this deeply searching, intensely personal type of writing, he would have become a totally different writer from the Galsworthy we know. As his books progress he acquires skill as a craftsman; *The Man of Property*, undoubtedly his most accomplished novel, has none of the naïvety of *Jocelyn*, nor the melodrama that makes the early novel slightly ridiculous, but it lacks the intensely personal quality that makes *Jocelyn* unique among Galsworthy's writings.

It was as if the book had taken flight, it had left its cautious author behind, kicking his well-bred, public school manners in the teeth, and in so doing saying things that its author did not mean to say, about himself, about Ada. In the future he would keep a guard over himself, but a guard is death to a writer; a writer must be reckless, he must let his imagination go where it will, say what it will. It was this lack of recklessness in Galsworthy's writing that enabled his avant garde contemporary, Virginia Woolf, to shrug him off at his death as "that stuffed shirt".

Jocelyn, with all its faults, reveals an aspect of John Galsworthy of which most of his readers are entirely ignorant. He was a passionate, warm, vital human being; and as we read his later more restrained novels it is well to remember that *Jocelyn* still lurks behind the pages.

Part I

Chapter One

A LIGHT laugh came floating into the sunshine through the green shutters of a room in the Hôtel Milano. It grated on Giles Legard, who sat on the stone terrace outside, face to face with a naked fact for, perhaps, the first time in ten years. He uncrossed his legs, finished his coffee, and rose listlessly, looking down the dried river bed towards the smooth sea. He was alone with the sunlight, and it laid bare his face with a convincing stare. The indifferent, gentle egotism of the man had recoiled before the meaning of things for so long, that the reality painted itself upon him harshly.

His long, sun-browned face had taken back momentarily its original pallor, his grey eyes were contracted, his square chin and jaw thrust forward doggedly; the thin curve of his dark moustache seemed to droop more than usual, and the lines of weariness round his mouth and eyes were deepened, till ridge and furrow were stamped as on a coin. His figure, tall and well knit, looked very lean and listless.

Yet, he had awakened to the dominating fact that he had blood in his veins—an overwhelming torrent of blood that sang in his head and throbbed in his hands, at a touch, that mastered his reason and his will, at a look. He was changed, absolutely changed, so that he felt he did not know himself any longer, that his outward manner alone remained to him—the merest superficial manner, standing as the only bar to revelations the depth of which he was now attempting to sound.

The more effectually to cast the lead in the uncertain waters of reality, he crossed the terrace abruptly and leant against the half-opened French window of a large room, in the screened corner of which a woman, dressed in white, was lying in a long invalid chair, reading, and making pencil notes. She looked up as his shadow fell across the light.

"Ah! Giles, I have not had the fortune to see you greatly to-day. Will you perhaps have the goodness to give me the little green book lying on that table? Do not stay, *je n' suis pas bon compagnon.* It does not go well, so that I just lie and read my Tolstoi."

Her pale, sallow face lighted up with a smile of thanks as he put the book within her reach.

"Have you been amusing yourself to-day, *mon cher?* Presently you shall tell the little English friend I should like to see her."

"Jocelyn is in the next room," said Giles slowly.

"Ah! but not now, I have so much pain just now. Give her my love, and tell her—later." Her black eyes from out of their hollows glanced half pitifully, half maliciously, at her husband, and then drooped resignedly with a quiver of bodily pain under brows that fell obliquely away from the furrow in the centre of her low Slav forehead.

"I'm very sorry that you're so ill to-day. Can I do anything for you?" said Legard. It was all he found to say, and his face in the maze of his emotions expressed no one of them.

"Amuse yourself, *mon cher*, I have no want of anything, except to be alone, this is one of my bad days, you know."

Again she looked at him, and, but for the pain of the whitened lips, one would have said she laughed. Giles turned away, but stopped at the window irresolutely; he had found no help. Irma Legard dropped her book with a slightly impatient gesture. A gleam of sun stealing round the screen fell on her face—she sat up, drew the screen forward, and sank back on her cushions with a sigh. The sound of a piano came from the next room.

"I beg your pardon," said Giles, "I am going," and stepped into the sunshine.

Through the green shutters of the adjoining room came a little petulant tune; Giles stopped, and his face quivered; the little tune gripped some string in his heart, it was as if the player had put her finger upon it, and pulled it towards her. He stood there leaning against the wall, with his hands in his pockets, and half-closed eyes. He had found the depth of those uncertain waters; they were just of that depth, whatever it might be, that mattered nothing. The reality of circumstance, of social relations and duties, no longer existed, *they* had become shadows to him; that which was real, the only thing which had substance, was the girl playing that tune in the shuttered room. Nothing else mattered. He had a momentary feeling of relief, the feeling which comes to the man whose life has been a compromise with circumstance, who has always been afraid of stretching out his hand too far, when, for the first time, he is conscious that his power of temporising has been taken from him—that in his life, it is to be all, or nothing. Shikari, the great brindled greyhound lying against the wall, paused in his occupation of lazily snapping at flies, and stretched himself to lick his master's hand.

"Amuse yourself, *mon cher!*" His wife's words came into Legard's mind, and he laughed. He did not find things amusing.

The green shutters were opened gently, and a man stepped on to the terrace.

"How do you do, my dear Legard?" he said in slow, suave, purring tones, putting on a soft, grey hat; "how very fortunate to see you. I am just off, you know."

Scrupulously dressed after the manner of the English, Gustavus Nielsen was unmistakably a foreigner. He was by birth a Swede, by education and adoption a Cosmopolitan. About forty years old, of medium height and substantial build, he carried a flaxen head stiffly upon his broad shoulders. His pale, sandy face, of a square moulding, was marked with innumerable little lines; one of two unfathomable eyes of a warm, reddish brown, was protected by a gold-rimmed eye-glass; and his tawny moustache curled walrus-like downwards to the level of his jaws. He carried under his arm a white, green-lined umbrella.

The two men shook hands; in the looks they exchanged was all the antagonism of an unconfessed rivalry.

"How goes the 'system'?" said Legard. It was the most dis-agreeable thing he could think of at the moment.

"Thank you," said the other, his face immovable. "Pretty well, pretty well, but we 'other' gamblers never mention it; we are afraid, don't you know. By the way, how is your dear wife? Give her my compliments. I am so sorry not to see her. I have been calling on Mrs. Travis and Miss Ley, and now I am afraid there isn't time."

Legard winced, he had got the worst of the exchanges.

"My wife is not very well, thank you. Good-bye, don't let me make you lose your train."

"Good-bye, my dear fellow," murmured Nielsen, putting up his green-lined umbrella, and disappearing at a slow, square walk in the direction of the railway station.

Left to himself, Giles returned to his moody, eager contemplation of the closed, green shutters. The afternoon sun streamed obliquely through the yellow sprays of a huge mimosa that hung balancing over the terrace wall, and the scent of roses and heliotrope was heavy on the faint puffs of air that came from the great tideless sea. Small brown lizards chased each other up and down the smooth walls of the hotel, and a mazy, shifting web of humming things and of butterflies wove itself over the stony waste of the terrace.

The domination of sex veiled all these things from Legard's senses. Something different, something unseizably different in the pressure of a girl's hand, and the world was changed to him.

Constitutionally lazy, constitutionally and unobtrusively egoist, he had come slowly to the realisation of the upheaval of foundations. It was too far, too foreign, too altogether strange. Yet, when it had come, it seemed to him the most natural thing to exchange a world of sun, of sweet sounds and scents, of colour, of resigned humdrum, of bored and gentle pleasure-seeking, for another world of fiercely passionate longing, of ache, of delight, of absolute absorption in the one idea—a world from which everything else was barred.

All that spring at Mentone he had accepted the one more beautiful thing that had come into his life, as for many years he had accepted the sun, the air, the flowers, the sea, everything that was fair in a very fair and pleasant land. *They* had become to him a part of his nature, so that he no longer wondered at them, and, Englishman though he was, gazed at the bewildered tourist with the mildly contemptuous surprise of the Southerner, to whom these things were the merest necessities of existence.

He had taken this one more beautiful thing as it came, without reflection, without thought, enjoying it day by day.

He had got into the way of taking things like this. Ten years ago, at the age of twenty-five, he had married a Polish lady, and had brought her soon afterwards, a confirmed invalid, to a villa on the Italian Riviera. They had never again moved far from it, it was too much trouble. His wife was always ill, she had her writing, her friends, her flowers. As for himself, he drifted along in an existence pleasant enough, which slowly and surely sapped his energy, and left him a sense of waste and of weariness that did not diminish with the passing years.

He had no particular ties with England. His father, a man of some position in his county, died from a fall out hunting when Giles was only four years old. The death of his mother, a very beautiful and good woman, came just as he was leaving Eton, and left a big mark upon his mind, strengthening the silent reserve of his nature; and yet even with her, to whom he had been devoted, he had never spoken of things which affected him deeply; it seemed as if the power of a complete trustfulness were hidden from him, and reserved for something fuller and more intimate to reveal.

At Oxford he made many friends, he was silently sympathetic to them, but when they came to sum him up, they were forced to confess that they did not know him, even in that ordinary degree in which youths know each other; they liked him, but they did not know him.

When he left Oxford, he was in the position of a man with no decided leanings or dislikes in regard to a profession, with more than sufficient means, and with a nature which required the spur of necessity or of some vital interest to force it to exertion. He spent some years in travelling, generally with sport as an object; and then came his marriage. He had never been quite able afterwards to understand how it had come about; it had been a matter of friendship, of sentiment, of compassion; but there it had been for ten years an accomplished fact, bringing with it a life from which all purpose seemed to be barred.

He had pursuits; for instance, he occasionally went over to Monte Carlo and gambled mildly, he made annual shooting trips to Algeria or Morocco, and he was continually yachting round the coast; but of work, nothing; of love—nothing!

There had never been anything really in common between him and his wife. Certainly, he was always gentle and courteous to her, but there was in her a vein of *spirituelle*, expansive *espiéglerie*, which was somehow beyond him; it did not hit with the grey and reserved temper of his mind, with his deeply-rooted indolence.

19

A man of refinement, of no vulgar instincts, of certainly the greater logical reasoning power, he had yet always found himself *un peu bête* in her presence, just a little commonplace—it was irritating.

He admitted to himself indeed, almost from the first, that his marriage had been a mistake, but he did not cease to have a great admiration for his wife's personality, for her courage and patience under suffering, for her wide sympathies, and the wit and charm of her manner. He regarded her with the eye of a stranger as a very desirable and delightful woman; he knew her to be the wrong one for himself.

He saw her side of the question also—it was a habit of his to see the other side—and he pitied her.

He frequently analysed the situation; it did no good, but it was natural to him.

Irma had never loved him, if she had, he would have given her love in return, for his nature was responsive and affectionate. As it was, he accepted the fact with gratitude. She had married him for one or other of the unnumbered reasons for which women marry men, any one of which is good enough till after the event.

The friction between their two natures was endless and incurable. It never found vent. It was never openly present, secretly never absent. Legard fell into the habit of taking things as they came, and cultivated the superficial philosophy of indifference. . . .

But now, standing in the sun, watching two closed green shutters, he found that philosophy an imperfect reed to his hand.

Chapter Two

EARLY frogs croaked in the *Val de Menton*, a fragrant acrid whiff of smoke from burning eucalyptus-wood floated up from the unkempt dwellings behind the hotel. The green shutters of the French windows were thrown back, and a girl appeared in the space between. She stood with her head slightly on one side, her hands in front of her, holding in them a branch of roses. As she twisted them to this side, and that, they reflected the sunlight through their pale yellow petals, hearts of orange, and ruddy-stemmed foliage, and gave a suggestion of gipsy colouring to her figure. She poised herself on the threshold of the window, with a little swaying motion like that of a bird upon a twig. Neither tall nor short, she had the indescribable quality of perfect proportion. From the soft, dark brown hair rippling back from her low forehead and drawn over the tip of the tiniest of ears, the arched instep thrust slightly forward under the folds of some soft, maize-coloured gown, the paramount impression conveyed was that of *race*—the subtle something which distinguishes the true Arab horse even from the English thoroughbred; the something very old, quite inseparable, ungrafted, which one may see in the purest gipsy types, the purest Arab or Persian; that something which produces an absolute uniformity of line and of "tone." The oval face in repose was stamped with a look of weariness, almost of sadness, an inherited look—as of one having played a game with fate and lost—which is seen so often in the Eastern, so seldom in the Western face. In the pallor of it was the slightest browning tint, the chance outcome of a long ago gipsy strain.

She smiled as she looked quickly about her with large, soft brown eyes, from under slightly arched, dark brows, and the lines of the mouth curved, and took to themselves two tiny dimples at the corners. There was no trace of the weary look in the face then; it was the very incarnation of light and life, as she sniffed the eucalyptus smoke luxuriously, and stretched like a little cat in the streaming sunshine. She gave a little nod to Giles, and stooped to pat the greyhound's head pushed up against her dress.

"Dear boy," she said softly, with the pretty childish lisp she used to her intimate beasts, "did 'oo want 'oor cake? I'll get him his cake, Giles." She turned back into the room, and came out again with two large slices of cake. She laughed while the dog ate them, and looked first at him and then at Giles, with friendly, untroubled eyes.

"Sweet boy! How he loves cake!" she said.

Giles had not moved; he stood with his hands in his pockets, leaning against the wall, and frowning from the sun in his eyes.

"Isn't it a heavenly day?" said the girl, "what a pity to have to go and spend hours in those stuffy 'Rooms'!"

"Must you go over to 'Monte'?" he said; "we might have gone a walk."

Jocelyn plucked a spray of the yellow mimosa, and held it up to see if it would go with the roses.

"Yes," she said, "it's such a pity; but Auntie's dying to go, and she won't go alone. The poor dear's got a new 'system.' She's been studying it all the morning, she doesn't understand it in the least, but that doesn't matter, you know, she always gives it up when it comes to the point. Are you coming over with us? Mr. Nielsen said he'd meet us in the Gardens." Giles bit his lips.

"Yes, I think so," he said.

Jocelyn took a long sniff of the roses, and walked up to the terrace wall. She stood there with her back to him, looking down on the white houses and the ill-kept gardens, where plants straggled, and coloured garments hung limply from lines. Presently, without turning her head, she put her hand on Giles's arm, and plucked his sleeve, saying—

"Look! What a wilderness! I believe I love even the untidiness of it; there's colour in it, anyway." Giles quivered when she touched him; he came close to her, and looked over her shoulder at the confused jumble of painted buildings, green foliage, and gay rags, with the blue sea shining beyond. With a thrill of delight he felt the touch of her shoulder against his arm.

"What a child it is for colour!" he said; "do you care so very much for the South?"

"I love it," she said, with a little sigh. She twisted her fingers in and out of each other in a way she had when she was thinking. "The only thing I don't care about are the people. I don't mean the natives, I don't know them, I mean hotel people; all the years I've been abroad, they're always the same, wherever one goes. This place is almost worse than any, because of Monte Carlo."

"Do you include me?" said Giles. She gave his coat sleeve a little friendly pull.

"Of course not; you're different, you don't seem to belong abroad at all." She turned her head slightly and looked at him. "In spite of your laziness, you are always in earnest, you see, Giles; you can't help being English all through."

"Ah!" said Giles, with a very faint smile, "it's nice to know one's always in earnest, isn't it, Shika?" And he stooped, and stroked the greyhound's nose.

"And you," he said, "what about you, Jocelyn?" She moved her supple body impatiently, and the look of defeat, which was never far away, came into her face.

"I am sometimes in earnest," she said slowly, "and sometimes not; it's always 'sometimes' with *me*, you know—I drift and drift." A brown lizard darted across the top of the wall almost under her fingers. Her eyes shone softly.

"Sweet little beast!" she said. "I wish I were a lizard, Giles; just to be in the sun all day, and bask, and never have anything to worry one, or to fight against." Giles, with his hands in his pockets, and his chin thrust forward, was looking at her hungrily.

"You would make a very decent little lizard, you are so quick," he said between his teeth, "rather too nice-looking, perhaps." He had to say something ridiculous to hide the tenderness that came into his voice. Jocelyn smiled; when she smiled her face was wonderfully soft, and the tiny dimples always came to the corners of her mouth; then she sighed.

"Oh dear! it must be nearly time to go. I would much rather stay with you, Shika," and the greyhound, who seemed to understand, licked her hand amicably with a wet tongue.

"Irma would like to see you—will you go to her for a minute?"

23

Giles brought out the words with difficulty.

"Of course I will." She moved quickly across the terrace to the window. Giles, still leaning against the wall, followed her with his eyes.

She knocked on the window softly, and passed through it. . . . That was a curious contrast in the dim, shaded room, into which the brilliant light filtered through the closed shutters—the dark-haired girl standing gracefully and pliantly erect in her yellow dress, shyly twisting the soft-petalled roses in her hands, and the shrunken, weary woman, in her white draperies on the couch, all the life that remained to her seeming to lie in her eyes alone; black eyes, with that peculiar mournful look seen in monkeys' faces, and yet with the steadfast faith of martyrs in them—eyes that differed from most, in that they were always alight, always expressionful.

To the immense physical difference between the two was added a vast disparity—that between the mind of disciplined and the mind of undisciplined impulse—and yet, each was conscious of a great liking, somewhat shyly expressed, for the other.

Irma had a free and unenvious admiration for the girl's supple life and beauty; Jocelyn could not help being attracted by the elder woman's wit, and she had a sincere compassion for her weary suffering. They had always a sense of pleasure in each other's company, though, in spite of having lived for two months in the same hotel, they had not seen much of one another. The Legards' villa was some five miles distant, but Mrs. Legard always wintered in Mentone to be near her doctor.

Jocelyn bent down over the couch, and laid the saffron-centred roses against the breast of the white dress.

"How good of you to bring me these," came in the softest, slightly-foreign, staccato English. "I am so glad to see you, I thought perhaps you would not be coming to-day, and I am going away, you know—has not Giles told you? Yes," and she laughed almost gleefully, "I have got my liberty from Dr. Lamotte; the spring cure is over, he cannot do any more for me now, it seems; so I may go back to my little villa, and my flowers and books, and my singing birds. I miss them so here. *Mon Dieu!* How I miss them! So, I am going to-morrow; but you will come and see me, will you not, Jocelyn? It is not far, you know, only about five miles. I will tell Giles he must bring you."

"Of course I will come, I want to see the villa so much, but I am sorry you are going."

"Yes?" The faintest mockery seemed to ring in the word, but she put out her hand, and took the girl's with a caressing gesture. "I do not like to ask your dear aunt; there is no roulette there, you know; she will perhaps be bored. Yes, I will tell Giles; he will bring you; I do not know if he is coming too—perhaps not." Again in the voice and the black eyes fixed so steadily on the girl's, there was that indefinable spirit of fleeting mockery; Jocelyn flushed slowly, her sensitive mind was aware of something unpleasant, which she did not understand. There was a light tap on the window.

"That is auntie," she said, "I must go, I'm afraid; we are going over to 'Monte.' "

"Good-bye, Jocelyn. Will you kiss me?" She gave the girl a look of mingled tenderness and admiration. "You are *so* pretty to-day."

Jocelyn stooped for a kiss.

"Good-bye! I am very sorry you are feeling so ill; shall I stay with you?" she said.

"*Mon Dieu!* No! The dear aunt would certainly be bored without you; you must go at once. *Bonne chance.* And you will come over and see me?"

"Yes," said Jocelyn. There was a troubled look on her face, as she turned it to the other before passing through the window.

Outside, Mrs. Travis's figure spread, straight and full, in a cool, grey silk gown, under a black sunshade.

She covered a good deal of ground. She had on a very smart bonnet, and large, easy boots; the keynote of her personality was struck in the words, "material comfort." It was an unconscious profession with her to pursue it, but she would have been the last to admit it. She was fifty, with soft, well-curled fair hair going grey, and hazel-green eyes; she had a good deal of colour. She was not a tall woman, but she impressed one as such, there was so much dignity about her—the dignity of the old Puritan stock—the dignity of obstinacy. She had no principle, or, rather, she had the principles of temporary convenience, and a lingering, superstitious remnant of a Puritan education, which compelled her against her desires to go to church on Sundays. She was fond of gambling; gambled badly and superstitiously, with a keen enjoyment; objected to people believing that she did so at all; suspected the "bank" of knowing too much when she lost; bore her losses, as she bore physical pain, with the stoicism of early education; expected the same stoicism, multiplied, in her niece. Without knowing it, she was a perfect mistress of the art of avoiding wrinkles.

If you scratch a Russian you come to a Tartar, if you scratch a human being you come to an animal; only in some cases you scratch more, in others less. In Mrs. Travis's case you scratched less. She suggested nothing so much as a large Persian cat.

With her bright, quickly-moving, greenish eyes she observed many things, conveying them as far as the shell which covered her reasoning powers—if she had any. She had much instinct, no logic.

She was frequently heard to say to her niece, "You ought to think of other people, my dear." And she did so herself—just so far as it suited her own convenience. She only said it to her niece in the impunity of close relationship; in other cases she became the sublime martyr in a smooth sulk. For the rest, she was entirely devoid of "inwardness," was hospitable, and a widow with no children, loved shopping and dress, collected silver, and did it all well and economically. She did not talk much, but smiled a great deal, a pleasant smile; when she was agitated she puffed her lips.

She puffed them now, saying to Jocelyn—

"We shall lose our train, my dear, and we ought to play before dinner, you know, I'm never so lucky after." She linked her arm in the girl's, and walked down the terrace steps, Giles following in a feeble endeavour to reconcile her bonnet with her boots. He was given to dissection, and Mrs. Travis was tough under the knife.

Chapter Three

JOCELYN LEY'S mother died when she was born. She was an only child, and her father, who was in the army, began immediately to idolise her with an abrupt and well-bred idolatry.

He came into some property shortly after his wife's death, and, leaving the service, took a place in the country, where he used to spend the winters in hunting. In the spring and summer he would go to London, or on a round of visits, sometimes taking Jocelyn with him. She grew up in rather a lonely way, with dogs and horses for her companions, and her education was of a desultory nature. She was a marvellously quick child, the joy and despair of her governesses, who were always exceedingly fond of her, and who found themselves perpetually obliged to leave at the most promising moments, because Major Ley wanted his daughter to be with him. She grew from a roundabout romp, who could never stay on her feet, and came continually to grief, into a slim sensitive girl, very easily hurt, shrinking like a tender plant from anything rough or unpleasant, with a love for animals, and an innate distrust of her own kind.

When she was eighteen her father died, leaving her independent, and very desolate.

In default of better things, he had entrusted her to his sister, for whom he had a certain contemptuous affection. The two ladies, marvellously dissimilar, got on fairly well together—perhaps because they never remained for long at a time in one place, perhaps because neither expected to understand the other, nor required much at her hands. They had spent most of the four years since Major Ley's death abroad, in Italy, Spain, Germany, and above all in Paris, which Mrs. Travis loved because of the garments to be obtained.

Jocelyn hated the grey monotony of English skies. She had a fierce love of the sun, of lands where the colouring hit the eye, where life *seemed* to throb with a fuller pulse.

From her mother, in whose family there was a tradition of gipsy blood, she had inherited a restless, moody nature, which ordained that she should wander, just as it decreed that she should be a slave to the ebb and flow of her emotions. She had a vast capacity for living in the passing moment, which indicated a nature very responsive to outward influences, and to her own physical condition.

In her, qualities, and the negations of those qualities, seemed to swing with a beat and recoil as absolutely weighed and regulated as that of a pendulum; they balanced each other in the scales of her mind. She herself recognised the perpetual equation, standing apart from her moods in a detached consciousness, regretfully indulgent, making no attempt to control or check, rather gauging them with a peculiar pessimism, a sympathetic insight, a tender desire to be good to herself. She extended this desire to all the world—she loved generously to appreciate and to be appreciated, investing herself thereby with a great quality of attraction, not lessened by the essential pride which forbade her to ask a favour from God or man. She never stirred a finger to attract admiration or affection, yet without appreciation she drooped as a flower without water. . . .

As the train droned sleepily on its way to Monte Carlo, she leant forward in the dust-coloured railway carriage to look at the curve of the bay between Cap Martin and Roquebrune. She was smiling unconsciously at the blue sea gleaming in the sunlight, the feathery, white edges of the tiny, tideless waves, the pine-clothed cliffs rising sheer behind the tail of the curving train, and the three sentinel palms on the rocky point in front. Giles sat opposite her, devouring her face with half-closed eyes. Once with an abrupt movement she touched his knees with her own; and then it wanted all of Mrs. Travis—expansive, leaning back, with hands folded on her lap, and quickly-glancing green eyes—to check the mad impulse suddenly aroused in him to take the girl in his arms. He spent all the rest of the journey in wondering if she knew of that touch.

They found Nielsen in the garden, fragrantly shaded by a pepper tree. He was sitting on a seat smoking a cigarette, and gravely contemplating the doings of a man, who resembled a Greek statue, and of a sheep-faced boy, who might have stepped out of one of Jean François Millet's pictures. These two seemed to be committed to the levelling of a heap of earth, which had been let fall from a cart drawn by a large, intelligent-looking mule; they continued, however, to seem, for they did absolutely nothing. Nielsen greeted the ladies with suave effusion; he was a devoted admirer of Jocelyn.

"Look at that man!" he said plaintively, pointing to the statue. "What a futile thing civilisation is! You know, I have seen much more energetic South Sea Islanders, and delightfully clean, except for palm oil, which, after all, is only soap. But look at that attitude! How beautiful! He has been leaning on his spade in six different attitudes, each more beautiful than the last, all this quarter of an hour, and now he is going to get himself a drink." For the statue moved away, and left the Millet boy to drag his weedy limbs and sheep-like face round and round the earth heap in a conscientiously monotonous, do-nothing shamble.

Nielsen continued. "He has no more anything than the Fijian, except clothes and dirt; and yet we have the habit of calling him a civilised being, and the other a savage, don't you see? It is all a matter of habit, you know."

He flicked the dust off his boots mournfully with a silk handkerchief.

Nielsen habitually gave people the impression of being affected; in reality he was not, it was in his case merely the grafting of the English manner upon the foreign; he impressed one as being cynical, in reality he was kind-hearted; he appeared to be mild, in reality he was explosive; he seemed to be continually dancing in attendance, in reality he was an original.

He was a man of good birth, and he had seen, in his forty years, a little of most things; he now lived by gambling on a "system." It said much for him that he still lived, and *well*. Many people who gambled themselves tabooed him for that reason, oblivious of the fact, that, to live in that way, requires a patience and self-possession wanting in nine hundred and ninety-nine people out of a thousand.

They walked together through the gardens up to the Casino. There is a subtly peculiar character about the Casino gardens at Monte Carlo. They are not indeed particularly beautiful—there are many more so—but there is a subdued and fragrant naughtiness about them, they are full of suggestion. The aroma, acrid and penetrating, vivid and enticing, of many unrestrained personalities seems to haunt them; in the midst of absolutely artificial surroundings one yet seems to revert to first principles, to those mysterious laws which make the world go round, hunting the ostrich of civilisation as it buries a lofty and well-intentioned head from the sight of its implacably eternal pursuers.

Presently they approached the Casino steps. Mrs. Travis was a little in advance, serenely conscious of good clothes, and puffing her lips in pleased anticipation. Jocelyn *distraite*, and slightly bored, walked with Nielsen, who chattered to her languidly, while Giles followed moodily behind.

In front of them strolled two Englishmen with a curiously jerky walk. Nielsen, commenting on them in a whisper to his companion, said gravely—

"Look, they are new arrivals—they have the Monte Carrlo walk —two steps and a scrratch, don't you know; all you English walk like that, you know, when you first come, it is the drry air."

Jocelyn smiled at him, and answered in low tones.

Giles, who had not caught the words of the whispered conversation, felt a sudden pang; he grew very pale, and dropped a little further behind. As Jocelyn went up the steps, she turned round and looked back for him.

The subdued strains of music came through the open doors of the concert-room; and in the outer hall and corridors people moved up and down with a prowling motion slightly suggestive of beasts at the Zoo; every now and then one would slip back again into the playing-rooms. Inside there was a hushed, jingling sound, a subdued light, a faint scent of patchouli. People shifted continually from room to room and round the tables, singly, or in groups of two and three talking in low voices. A ring of faces circled each table, and watchful croupiers at the ends and sides shepherded them apathetically with incessant energy. Their rakes clacked against coins on the green cloths, and the drawl *"rein n'va plus"* went continually up to the vault of the painted ceiling.

The endless motion of fans gave an impression of great insects hovering between the players. The faces were for the most part grave, there was no laughter; and the walls of the rooms stared baldly at them in bright colours, covered with painted nymphs; on couches, here and there, people sat, idly talking, or gazing wearily in front of them. Now and then a hum would swell up from one of the tables, and die down again into monotony.

Mrs. Travis, who always played roulette because it afforded her the luxury of more vacillation for her money, selected a table, and waited till she could sit down next to a friendly and clean Austrian croupier, whom she had habituated by a long and careful interchange of badly pronounced *"Bonjours"* to supervise the placing of her stakes. She proceeded to put purse, fan, and handkerchief beside her, and to take from her pocket pencil and cards whereon to mark the numbers. Her lips moved incessantly, her eyes glanced restlessly from the table to her cards and back again, and occasionally she gave quick looks at the players round—she seemed to see everything. She marked her cards carefully, consulted them much—fingered her stakes before placing them, often drawing them back at the last moment. When she won, she smiled—when she lost, she frowned; she was beautifully unconscious that she did any of these things. As she played, the lines deepened in her face, the colour faded—in short, she returned to first principles—a gambler pure and simple.

Jocelyn's proceedings were in curious contrast. She took the first empty seat. Her eyelids dropped, her chin tilted up, her face assumed a mask of indifference. She pushed her stakes on with the rake, carelessly, as if they did not belong to her, she raked them in carelessly in the same way. She backed her luck and cut her losses with nonchalance in an orthodox fashion—gambling because other people gambled.

Giles, standing at the same table, staked feverishly on every spin of the wheel. He kept his eyes all the time on Jocelyn. He won a good deal, put it in his pocket, and made a motion towards her, but, receiving no sign of invitation, went back to his place, and played with his eyes still upon her, till he had lost all he had with him. Then he turned away with an air of relief, and, going round, stood behind her chair, where now and again his coat sleeve would brush against her shoulder. He had played for a distraction without finding it.

Nielsen sat at a given table, watching the game; he looked sad, expressionless. He played from the marked cards in his hands and the figures in his head; he awaited combinations. He staked rarely, content with a five per cent. profit upon his outlay of the afternoon. Presently some one appropriated his stake—he looked at the man, mildly hurt, but said nothing; shortly afterwards some one appropriated his neighbour's stake—he at once exploded in defence; with words he cudgelled the appropriator, he cudgelled the croupiers, he brought the table about his ears, his face grew white, his eyes red, he held on to his point and gained it, then became once more sad and expressionless. For the rest he gambled undeviatingly—a mere matter of business.

Presently they came away, leaving Nielsen waiting patiently for a certain combination. As Jocelyn passed his chair he leant back, and twisted his rather short neck round to say, in a pathetic whisper, and with a shrug of his shoulders—

"*Ça ne va pas, ce soir,* I wait and wait, but the brread and butter does not come, and now you are going away, that is drreadful, don't you know." He had to twist back again in a hurry to mark his card with the last number.

Jocelyn, looking back, thought that he resembled a well-groomed seal watching a hole for fish.

Mrs. Travis, playing her new "system" with assiduous ignorance, had lost all her own money, had borrowed Jocelyn's, and lost that. She left the "Rooms" stiff with anger, erect, annoyed with her croupier, whom she believed capable of predicting the coming numbers if he would, strongly convinced that if she had brought more money she must have won, secretly ruffled with Jocelyn for not having more to lend her.

Very little was said on the return journey; Mrs. Travis's quick green eyes seemed restlessly on the watch for something to resent, Jocelyn was tired, Giles moody. Only when they neared the hotel, he touched her sleeve gently, saying—

"You know we are off to-morrow?"

"Yes," she answered, "I am so sorry."

She stopped, and a faint colour came into her cheeks.

"I shall miss our walks dreadfully, and Shika—poor boy: he won't get his cake. Will you remember to give it him every afternoon?"

"No," said Giles shortly, "I'll bring him over for you to give it."

"Oh!" she said, drawing little circles in the dust with the end of her parasol. He was standing in front of her, tall and straight, with his hat off, and a very grave face. She looked up at him quickly, and held out her hand with a smile.

"We are dining out," she said, "I don't suppose I shall see you again. Good-bye, Giles." He took her hand in his, and held it a moment, looking very hard into her face; then he let it go, and stood quite still while she climbed the terrace steps. She turned her head once, and he caught a side glimpse of a tired, rather sad, little face under a shady hat.

Chapter Four

THE Legards left Mentone very early the following day; it was necessary for Irma to drive the five miles to the villa in the cool of the morning. Giles had failed to see Jocelyn again; he delayed the departure as much as he could, but she was not down when they left. During the drive he sat silently calm opposite his wife, but with a feeling of rage and despair in his heart. He took the greatest care of her, changing her cushions continually, and making the man drive with the utmost caution. They arrived without incident. He had hoped that he would find some relief and distraction in the familiar surroundings of the villa, but he found instead that they only maddened him by bringing to his mind more forcibly the bar set between him and Jocelyn. He asked himself, a hundred times a day, what he was doing? what he meant to do? and he could give himself no answer. His conscience, his sense of balance, his honour, whatever name best fitted that feeling which struggled with his passion, exacted from him a dying remonstrance. He tried to give himself no time to think, to keep himself busy all day and every day, riding, walking, or with affairs in the house; he was particularly attentive to his wife, and he felt all the time that she knew what was passing in his heart; and all his efforts were of no use—Jocelyn's face was ever before him. He wrote a note to her, in which he said that he had business which would take him to Genoa. He went there, and stayed two days, at the end of which time he returned more miserable than ever. In this way a week passed without his going to Mentone.

Jocelyn missed him; she had become so used to his companionship in those two months. She had no idea, until he had gone, how much she had depended on him for enjoyment. She felt quite lost without him and the greyhound. He seemed to her so different from the men, Germans, Frenchmen, Poles, or Russians with whom she had been thrown during her wanderings. They had danced with her, ridden with her, paid her compliments, even asked to marry her, and one and all she had distrusted them, with the native distrust peculiar to her. She had always felt as if she understood Giles. It was not because he was her countryman, it was for no defined reason; yet it had been good to be with him; to find some one who loved, like herself, the sun and the flowers, music, the hot, sweet-scented air, the clack of many foreign tongues in the glowing light, and on starry evenings the murmur of the deep-hearted sea. To know that there was some one near who felt the spirit moving in these things, who lived in them, to whom they were not, as to her aunt, merely the chance outside ministers of a bodily ease. . . . After he had gone, she would sometimes go into the garden with her lips pursed up in a dumb whistle, expecting every minute to see Shikari uncoil his snake-like body from under the shade of some shrub, and come lolloping across the grass with arched back to lick her hands; or to see Giles sitting in the sun with a Panama hat over his eyes, and his long legs crossed. Sometimes, as she sat indoors alone, or with her aunt, she would fancy she smelt the smoke of his cigar on the terrace, and she would get up and look through the shutters. She ceased to go for walks—it was so dull by herself, and she no longer cared to go over to Monte Carlo. She played to herself a good deal, but she found that she missed Giles's grave face looking at her, and a habit, which he had, of coming up from behind and touching her on the shoulder, saying, "Play that again." She wanted somebody to like her music. It was no good playing when there was nobody to care whether she played badly or well.

When she received his note she was surprised, and a little hurt, not at the news it contained, but at the wording—it seemed to her so formal and precise.

She sat down, and wrote him a friendly letter in return, then tore it up in a sudden fit of childish irritation, and wrote to Irma instead, telling her what a good time she was having.

Just a week after the Legards had gone, she found herself with

Mrs. Travis at a party given by a certain German baroness at her hotel in the East Bay. The hot, airless rooms, opening into each other, were filled with a cosmopolitan crowd of people, raising a gabble of words and laughter. The majority of them discussed the health of themselves and of their friends; a German professor, sitting at the piano, now and then struck a chord upon it to illustrate an argument he was carrying on; a fat, brown poodle begged incessantly, all over the room, for cakes; in a corner two Russians with parted beards disputed in low tones over a "system"; and an old English lady, stolidly eating an ice, complained of toothache to a Colonial bishop, who stood beside her with his hat clasped to his stomach. On the gravel walk outside, people paraded vaguely, smelling at the flowers, or turning to stare at new arrivals. There were present, in fact, all the ingredients of hotel society on the Riviera.

Mrs. Travis, seated in a cool corner of the room, was fanning herself, and listening with an occasional ample wriggle to the conversation of an anæmic curate, who was endeavouring to expound his own, and to elicit her views upon art. Having no views, she was finding it best to agree with everything he said, while her quick eyes took in a large amount of information about the dress and appearance of her neighbours. She smiled a great deal at him, however, so that he was quite pleased—considering himself appreciated—and presently brought her some tea.

In the centre of the room a knot of people surrounded Jocelyn, two of them talking to her eagerly in spasmodic and heavy-shouldered sentences; they were both Germans—Jocelyn had a peculiar fascination for Germans, they came round her like flies round honey. One of them would say—

"Do you that gomposer zo much like, ach?" The other: "Has he not veeling, ach?" and Jocelyn contrived always to convince each of them that she had answered him first. She did not wish to attract them, but only to avoid hurting their feelings. She appeared delicious to them, with her vivid yet mysterious face, and the absolute daintiness of her gestures and her dress. Every now and then she turned to the only other lady in the group, and tried to draw her into the talk, and, curiously enough, she seemed delicious to her also, having the faculty, given to a few attractive women, of not arousing the jealousy of her own kind. The Germans were pressing her to play, and she was turning to the piano when her eyes fell upon the figure of Giles. He was standing outside one of the French windows with his hands in his pockets, watching her. She gave an abrupt little movement, and sat down at the piano feeling suddenly hot. She began turning the leaves of some music hastily, with the idea, without knowing why, that she must hide her eyes from people. She played a mazurka of Chopin's, while the German professor, leaning over, regarded her admiringly through his smoked spectacles. When she had finished, she got up, saying, in answer to a buzz of remonstrance, "It's too hot to play," and walked away to a chair, with a sudden impatience of the people around her. She was thinking, "Why doesn't Giles come and talk to me?" The German professor, who had followed her from the window, began a commentary upon composers; Jocelyn, leaning back in her chair, listened languidly, while her eyes wandered to the window. A tall, good-looking woman in pink was talking to Giles, who was listening with a smile on his face. Jocelyn wondered who she was, and made an absent remark to the professor. She observed the look of mild surprise that lurked behind his spectacles, and caught herself up with her habitual quickness; but the moment he began to talk again her eyes went back to the window. Giles, bending a little forward, was holding the curtain aside to allow his companion to pass into the open air. Jocelyn felt a kind of dismay, as if something unpleasant and unexpected had happened.

"*Und* Schubert," the German professor was saying, "how *wunderschön mit* his beaudiful melodies, *nicht wahr*!"

"Ah!" she answered shortly, with her eyes on the ground, "I don't like him at all, he is too sweet," and was surprised at her own irritability.

When she looked up again she met Giles's eyes. He stopped short in the act of stepping through the window, and she felt as if something were passing from him to her in that look. Without glancing again, she knew that he was threading his way towards her, and the colour began to come slowly into her cheeks. She plucked incessantly at a loose thread in her skirt, and talked nervously. When he came up she held out her hand to him with a smile; he took it silently in his, and stood close to her, without joining in the talk. She felt suddenly light-hearted, and began a gay and laughing discussion with the professor. They disputed upon the colouring of the Riviera. The professor, a short, bearded man, with a square finger, prominent blue eyes, and a red face, maintained that it was too vivid.

"Dere is no zoul in it, no veeling, *nicht wahr?*" he said, "everydings you zee at once—it is not inderesding."

"Ah! But always to have the sun, and the beautiful clear sky, what does anything else really matter except that, Herr Schweitzer? Besides, there are the olives—isn't there any soul in them?"

"Ach! The olives, dey are ingongruous, like a grey goat on an Idalian beasant. I like more de zcenes mit de bine woods, und de rivers vlowing, und to zee de beasts und de women in de vields."

"Yes, I like that too, but I don't feel as if I *lived* there, you know, as one does in the South."

"*Ach! Mein fräulein*, you are English; like all de English you will eggzitement have. For me to dake his ztick and walk in de beaudiful woods und vields, und to zee nadure, und den berrhaps to rest, und drink a liddle beer, and walk again, dat is 'abbiness—ach!'"

He beamed at her sentimentally through his spectacles. At this moment Mrs. Travis approached; she was greatly bored by her curate, and by the heat, and wished to depart. Giles, with a look of relief upon his face, went out to find their carriage; in spite of his yearning to be with Jocelyn, it tortured him to see her talking to other people. He had come to the party in the hope of finding her, proposing just to look at her, and to go away. As he put them into their carriage, her hand rested lightly on his arm, and she said—

"When are you coming over to see us, Giles?"

"To-morrow," he answered, trembling all over. He did not take his eyes from her face, and when she looked back at him as the carriage drove away, she felt again as if something were passing between them.

"*Au revoir!*" she cried, waving her hand. All the way home she felt curiously light-hearted. . . .

After dinner that evening, she wandered alone into the hotel garden; the endless chatter of the drawing-room irritated and annoyed her—she wanted to be alone.

The night was breathlessly still, the scent of roses and heliotrope hung heavily in the air, fire-flies flashed, and now and then a blue gleam of the summer lightning rent the clear dark. For a moment the silence was intense, then suddenly a frog croaked harshly, the cry of a peacock or a far-off shout from the street broke the stillness and died away. Jocelyn walked up and down one of the paths, and then stood looking into the night with soft eyes. Her lips parted in a caress. . . . What a marvellous world under those remote and silent stars! If she could but take it into her arms and kiss it! Kiss the sweet flowers, the still air, the whole wonderful night! It seemed more to her than ever before—fuller of meaning and of delight. She stretched out her arms, and then pressed them to her breast with a sudden irresponsible motion of which she was half ashamed. . . .

The light of a lamp streamed from an open window into the darkness, and stretched in a band of gold over the dew-stained grass. Jocelyn turned away; it seemed to her like a hot and intruding touch upon the purity of the night. She drew a long breath of the warm air, feeling utterly and unreasoningly happy—as if nothing could touch her, as if her steps were guided by some soft gleam shining mysteriously from behind the curtain of life. She did not seek to know why she had that strange and sweet sensation; it was enough for her that she felt the throb of the stars, the dumb whisper of the dreaming night. She pressed the backs of her hands against her cheeks—they were glowing as if from kisses. . . .

The hoarse barking of a dog rose from the distant street; with a faint rustling the quiet garden seemed to stir resentfully, as though some strange breath had stolen into it. Jocelyn gave a little shiver, she twisted with her hands the muslin scarf around her neck and shoulders—it was all limp and wet with the dew. With a sudden feeling of discouragement she turned and went back into the house.

That night she lay awake a long while, thinking.

Chapter Five

GILES rode over the next morning. He found Jocelyn and Mrs. Travis in the garden of the hotel talking with a young Englishman. They came forward to meet him, but he felt at once that in Jocelyn's greeting there was something foreign to her, something almost repellent. After the first moment she did not look at him; all her attention seemed bestowed upon the speech of the young Englishman, who stood, speckless, descanting upon "systems," the demerits of which he illustrated languidly with his fingers. He was a weakly, immutable young man, sloping from the crown of his head to the soles of his feet. He began it with his forehead, and continued it all the way down; his voice sloped—it came out of him loudly, and died away; his hands sloped—they began large, and ended small. He never smiled—not from set purpose, but because he had lost the art, and his eyes calculated continually out of the monotony of a colourless face.

" 'Systems' are all rot," he was saying, "there are only two fellers in Monte Carlo who make it pay, don't y' know, old Blore and Nielsen; an' they don't do it by figures, only by bein' so 'nfernally patient."

Mrs. Travis, sitting upright in a cane chair with her hands in her lap, listened with attentive disapproval; she had a "system," and did not wish to be convinced of its inefficiency.

"But I watched Baron Zimmermann myself, and I saw him win five hundred louis the day before yesterday, he plays a 'system,' I know," she said.

"Lost it all yesterday, and more," said the young man dispassionately. It was his *métier* to know everything about everybody, for which reason Mrs. Travis respected him.

"But perhaps he wasn't playing his 'system' then," she said.

"Why not?"

"Oh, I don't think he would be," a remark which was a fair specimen of her methods of discussion. She never believed what she did not want to, and rarely anything that she did not see with her own eyes.

"Figures are against you, y've only got one thing in your favour, don't y' know," said the young man languidly; "you c'n leave off playin' when y' like, and the bank has to go on." His voice ran into a whisper, and he tilted his hat till it sloped down the back of his neck.

Giles stood a little way from them, watching Jocelyn eagerly. He caught her looking at him two or three times with eyes that seemed to be asking a question—eyes that were full of trouble and uncertainty. He could not understand the change in her; recalling the friendly serenity of the parting look she had given him the day before, he wondered with a secret dismay. He went up to her and said—

"Will you come and look at the pony? You said you wanted to see it."

"Yes," she answered indifferently, and walked away with him to the stables, leaving the young man caressing the slope of his moustache, and calculating into vacancy. On the way to the stables she hardly talked at all, only answering in monosyllables when he spoke to her; every now and then she would look at him stealthily, with that same expression of perplexity and fear. As she stood talking to the pony, with her arms round its neck, her cheeks laid against its mane, and her eyes soft under their long lashes, Giles felt an uncontrollable rush of longing to be near her, to touch her, and share in the tenderness of her voice and her face. He came close, and laid his hand partly over hers upon the pony's head. She drew it away quickly with a look of positive fright, and the colour rushed furiously into her face. He looked at her silently, and he could not keep the pain and hunger out of his eyes. She went on mechanically stroking the pony's neck. At last he said, rather because his feelings fought for expression than that the words were those he wished to speak, "What's the matter, Jocelyn? Why

41

do you treat—?" She stamped her foot upon the straw of the stall, and without saying a word, went out of the stable. He stood there, biting his moustache, dumb with pain and dismay, and the pony thrust its wet nose against the pocket of his coat. He recovered himself a minute later, but she had gone to her room, and though he waited a long time, he did not see her again, and at last went away, half distracted with doubt and fear. . . .

After that, his will made no further remonstrance. All that he thought of, day and night, was to be near her. Conventional morality ceased to be anything to him but a dim, murky shadow, falling at times across the path of his longing. He was face to face with two very grim realities, gaunt and shadowless, which hurt him, bit into his soul, absorbed his consciousness—his great unslaked thirst, and his dread of bringing her harm. He was unable to see issues clearly outlined under the pressure of the throbbing passion which possessed him. All that was highest in him was roused, all the self-sacrifice of which he was capable, all the desire to be of use, of protecting use, to some other human being; and by a grim irony it was aroused by that very implanted impulse in his sensuous fibre to be at one with that other, to be all in all to her, to rend the veil which divided her from him, body and soul. He thought of her reverently, as something sacred and unstained, yet he would have given ten years of his life to put his lips to hers. His will, undermined by years of easy drifting with the tide, made feeble attempts to grapple with the end; painfully achieved resolutions, painfully abandoned them, finally confessed dimly that he could neither give her up nor do anything to bring her harm.

So possessed, he made daily pilgrimage from the sunlit Italian villa into Mentone, and every day a rising tide of passion left him a step higher upon a thirsty beach of thankless indecision.

Shikari, the greyhound, who shared with him the daily journeying, and who slept by his bed at night, was the only living thing that gave him some comfort during those days when his old easy life slipped away from him. Jocelyn's great love of animals invested the dog with an added attraction. Something of herself, Legard thought, seemed to stay with the caresses and the sweet words she had lavished upon him.

There was, besides, a sense of comradeship in the touch of the brute's muzzle against his knee, which no human being could give, while his mind was kicking, impotently and incessantly, against the pricks of humanly-ordained circumstance. He managed to keep a certain hand upon his actions; he remained calmly and wearily gentle to his wife, but often when he looked at her, he would awake suddenly to consciousness that he was trying to measure the ebbing vitality in her face and gestures, and he would turn away hating himself. Every morning he started from the villa, and walked the five dusty miles westwards under the blazing sun with a swinging, hardly restrained stride; every night he came slowly and listlessly back, under cover of the dewy darkness, his face drawn and his lips working. He used to walk both ways, so that in weariness he might get some freedom from thought at night. He did not always see Jocelyn. Sometimes his courage would fail him at the last moment, and he would not even make the attempt, but would hang about the town utterly wretched, and go back at night cursing his cowardice. It was a part of his misery too that he could not understand her. Some days she would hardly speak to him, would shrink if by accident he touched her, and avoided being alone with him; at other times she would seem as friendly and serene as in the old days; but even then she left the impression upon him, that she had been forcing herself not to think and feel, simply to live in the passing moment. She never touched him if she could help it, and her eyes seldom met his; by virtue of her woman's quickness, they fell soft and luminous under the veil of their dark lashes before he could read the meaning in them. And he knew that it was all his own fault—for, do what he would, he could not hide his feelings. At times he was cold to her, almost sullen, at others quite silent; sometimes he could not keep back the tenderness in his voice, then again he would be suddenly conventional and abrupt, and always—always—he looked at her with hunger in his eyes. When he saw her in the presence of other people he suffered tortures of jealousy, he wanted her ever to himself. That expression of shrinking, almost of horror, in her face, haunted him; sometimes he would go away, cursing himself, calling himself a brute, and a beast, for bringing her a moment's pain— he would even resolve to give her up and never see her again; but to no end—he could not keep away. Once, when she thought herself unobserved, he saw her looking at him with an expression in her eyes that he had never seen before—an expression in which wonder, fear, pity, and something very deep, were strangely blended; his heart leaped within him, but the next moment the look was gone, and her face was mysterious and inscrutable as a mask. He lived upon that look for days.

In his mind he perpetually reviewed all the unconsidered trifles of their meetings, the words spoken, and the words that seemed to hang unspoken on her lips, the thoughts that showed in her face and the thoughts unimaged, unconfessed—and neither her woman's instinctive dissimulation, nor the greatly unconscious, greatly untested barrier of a girl's reserve, could hide them altogether from his despairing eyes. He searched as a thirsty man seeks water in a desert, where to find it is life—to fail death. The knowledge that he was staking his all in that search, and yet that, even if he found it, it must needs be brackish, perhaps undrinkable, gave him a keenness of vision denied to most lovers' eyes. As the days ran into weeks he grew tired and worn-looking, and hollows began to come into his sun-burnt face. He lived, knowing nothing with certainty, nothing of what she felt, nothing of what he desired, nothing of the end. He lived a prey to hunger and to doubt. . . .

One morning, as he was coming up to the hotel, he encountered Mrs. Travis, setting forth upon her daily visit to Monte Carlo. She told him that Jocelyn had taken a book, and gone for a walk by herself. He accompanied the good lady to the station, and watched her train go out, then he took the nearest way through the outskirts of the town to a sloping ridge which he knew to be Jocelyn's favourite walk. The sun blazed fiercely, and in the town the heat brooded breathlessly over the houses, over the streets, and the dried watercourses. He passed a company of soldiers, in blue jackets and white trousers, straggling dustily along the road; three or four little girls on donkeys clattered by him laughingly, bumping up and down and chattering incessantly, while the drivers followed, flourishing sticks.

In the narrow lane of the steep ascent wild roses hung in clusters from the hedges; and now and then he passed unkempt cottages whence came the smell of burning wood and the barking of dogs. He came out at last upon a ridge, running between two terraced, vine-grown valleys. The uncertainty of his quest gave him courage, and he walked rapidly without dwelling upon the thought whether or not she would be glad to see him; but he had almost given up hope, and was about to retrace his steps, when he suddenly caught sight of her sitting on a bank of thyme, a little way down the left hand slope. Her elbows rested on her knees, and her chin was sunk

44

in her hands; a book lay open by her side. His heart gave a great leap, and beat painfully; he stood still, doubting what he should do, but the sudden ceasing of footsteps had attracted her attention, and she looked up. He lifted his hat.

"May I come? Or shall I go back?" he said.

She looked at him startled, half rising from the ground.

"Shall I go away?" he repeated.

"It would be better," she said; and then, as if to recall the strange words, she held out her hand and said—

"Oh, no! Come, of course, if you like."

He went down the slope, dry and slippery under his feet, and threw himself at full length close to her. In the valley below the almond trees were flushing in the sun; on the hillside the olives glistened, here and there a tall cypress stood like a sentinel over the scene, and pine trees crowning the ridge behind seemed to climb towards the blue of the sky. Cuckoos were calling, bees droning, and the tinkle of cow-bells floated up the valley. Little flowers pushed their tiny heads up around, and in all the still air was the scent of the thyme.

"This is the hour I love best," said Jocelyn, "when the day is just sleeping; resting after its climb, before it begins to go down hill again. Listen to the bees, what a lullaby!"

She held up her finger, and sat with her head bent a little to one side, and a smile on her lips. Giles watching her, as always, saw the smile fade, leaving her face weary and troubled. He took up her book, and began turning over the leaves, with the feeling that by the trivial action he was warding off the pain which he felt was coming. Suddenly, she said—

"What does the world want with people? They only spoil it! It is *so* beautiful, except for our horrible, horrible selves."

She put her hands out, as if she would push away from her something weighty and oppressive. The motion went straight to his heart; he sat up with an abrupt movement, and turning half away from her, clenched his hands; feelings of grief and rage tore at him.

Presently he felt a soft pull at his sleeve. He looked at her. The little oval face, with its large brown eyes, was so pathetic that all bitterness left him, and he thought only of how to bring the light back into it. He began to talk about the book, about anything that came uppermost in his mind, and gradually the old friendly serenity came into her face. They sat there a long time, talking and reading, while the shadows of the pine trees lengthened, and in the slanting sun the light mellowed on the hillside. At last Jocelyn said—

"It's time for me to go back."

She was rising to her feet, when her foot slipped, and she fell nearly to the ground. Giles standing close caught her in his arms. He felt her breath on his cheek, the soft pressure of her yielding body against him—and his eyes blazed with the sweet emotion that leaped up in his heart. When she was on her feet again, he held her for one second. Suddenly her frame became rigid, she pushed him violently away from her, and covering her face with her hands, turned, and almost ran up the slope. Giles stood where she had left him, motionless....

Half an hour later he too went up the slope. At the turning into the lane, Jocelyn rose from the trunk of a fallen tree on which she had been sitting, and came up to him without a word. Her face was flushed, there were circles beneath her eyes, and he knew that she had been crying. With a catch in his breath, he took her hand and stroked it gently. They went down the hill together silently.

Chapter Six

GILES paced up and down his verandah restlessly; he was await-
ing Jocelyn's arrival. His wife had sent an invitation to her and to
Mrs. Travis to come and see the villa, with the suggestion that
they should afterwards drive on to Bordighera. Nielsen, who had
also received an invitation, was coming with them; the prospect
of a whole day of Jocelyn's society having caused him for once
to abandon his professional visit to the gambling-tables.

The little grey villa hanging over the Cornice road smiled
down a sheer descent at the sea, which danced, far out, to the tune
of the breeze in lines of sapphire, and, shorewards, was ringed
smoothly with a dull, turquoise crescent of water, broken only
where the foam-scud, shining in the brilliant sunshine, flew up
over the green-grey rocks. Below the wall, on the nether side of
the road, a clump of silver olives swayed gracefully in the
freshening breeze, and beyond, a group of stone pines brooded,
thoughtful and apart, at the edge of the cliff. Hanging masses of
pink geranium, and wine-coloured bougainvillea stained the
greyness of the villa walls, and rainbow roses clung in festoons
round its closed, green shutters.

Up the curved, white vista of dusty road toiled the figure of an
old man, sturdily bending under his load of palm branches. A
two-horsed cart rattled noisily downwards towards the bridge to
the crack of the driver's lash and his shrill "yuips." Just in front
of the villa three small brown urchins chattered busily in the dust,
heaving flat stones aimlessly along the road; and the soft, metallic

note of women's talk, with a wailing rise at the end of each sentence, floated up from a gaily-skirted group washing linen in the tank below. To the left, where the road wound past a buttress of old grey masonry, palms clustered skyward in dusty profusion; to the right, through a slanting, mauve network of wisteria and sleepy heliotrope, one caught a glimpse of the lichen-dotted wall of a Saracen tower, rising solid and picturesque, pierced in the centre by a white-washed stone archway. The sea gave a blue-green setting to the spreading foliage, to the gnarled trunks of the balancing olives and the stems of the pines; the edging foam, glinting white as it shot up over the rocks, seemed to throw a playful challenge to the friends that had hung so long above in airy seclusion.

In a corner of the garden, where a pepper tree threw feathery shadows from its hanging, frond-like leaves, and dull pink berries, on to the grass, Shikari lay, his head between his paws, watching his master's restless figure out of one half-closed eye.

Presently the sound of wheels was heard coming up the road. Giles stopped his uneasy tramp on the broad verandah, and, followed by the dog, went and stood at the top of the crescent of trellis-roofed steps, that led curving up to the door from the outside porch. The carriage stopped. Jocelyn was the first to alight. She stood, for a minute, before she mounted, looking up at him through the roses which trailed mysteriously over her head out of shadowy masses of hanging foliage—falling through the openings of the twisted trellis-work, they seemed to be whispering and beckoning to her, as she stood under the green archway.

Shikari walked gravely down the steps, and raising himself, placed a paw on each of her shoulders.

Irma was waiting for them in a cool room on the ground floor. She looked very ill, but she greeted her visitors with graceful cordiality. Giles noticed that she looked at Jocelyn with a strangely wistful expression. Nielsen, who had followed them into the room, suddenly produced from his pocket a beautiful little china bowl, which he presented to his hostess with his usual elaborate languor.

"I have been waiting for the chance of giving you this, my dear lady," he said, bowing. "It was presented to me by my dear frriend Dick Garron; it comes from Yokohama, you know; I have beeen tortured," and he spread his hands expressively, "for fear it should be destrroyed by my cats. I should not feel it so deeply, don't you see, if it were destrroyed by *other* people's cats."

Irma's tired face, yellow-white from constant pain, lighted up with a smile. Jocelyn had brought her flowers, Mrs. Travis, chocolate; the three characteristic gifts touched her fancy humorously. As she murmured her gracious, foreign thanks, her eyes—like those of a souled monkey—kept glancing from Jocelyn as she put the flowers in water, to Giles, who leant against the door watching her. He caught one look from his wife; there was such sadness, such depth of comprehension, such mockery in it, that he knew once for all there was nothing to hide from her. He dropped his eyes, and there was a moment when his feelings were a strange mingling of shame, regret, bitterness, and compassion —a moment of absolute physical discomfort; then he stepped across, smoothed her cushions, and with a muttered excuse left the room.

Nielsen, an old friend with a great and sympathetic admiration for the sick woman, had much to say, and proceeded to say it. Mrs. Travis was busy inspecting the silver in two cabinets against the wall, examining the pattern critically, and murmuring a constant approval. Jocelyn, left to herself, talked to two bullfinches, who instantly became her friends. Her nerves were on edge, the strain of the situation, whether she would or no, was being forced upon her reason. Her aunt's complacent comments, Nielsen's languid chatter, Irma's eyes so full of meaning and knowledge, and yet so kind, jarred her. The colour came and went in her face, and her eyes looked restlessly about her; she revolted impatiently in a hardly-repressed irritation against the confinement of the pretty, dainty room, shaded by the verandahs from the powerful beat and throb of life outside. She longed to get into the sunshine, away from the thoughts that crowded painfully upon her mind.

She felt an immense relief when Giles's voice summoned them to the carriage, and she went out and drew a deep breath, with Irma's farewell words sounding in her ears—

"Good-bye, dear one, you are young and so beautiful; have a good time, it is right, it is fitting." ...

To the jingling of their ear bells, the pair of little flea-bitten greys raised a whirling column of dust on the winding, downward road to Ventimiglia. With every step gained from the villa, Jocelyn's spirits rose in the rapid motion through the warm dry air; she lost herself in the brilliant day, in the passing glimpses of the laughing sea, in the hot pine scent from above the road. She shook her parasol gaily, with a smiling *"Buon Giorno,"* at a group of Italian peasant girls swinging along, slowly and erect, to market; the flowers which she had tied round its handle swayed and quivered, sending their perfume over to Giles, who sat opposite her. She did not look at him; it seemed as though she had determined to forget everything—everything but the throb of the warm life that stirred around her.

As they rose a slight hill, they passed a man with a gun slung over his shoulder by a strap. Side-whiskered, with a hard felt hat and a nondescript dog, he was going out to shoot singing birds.

"Le sport!" said Giles, with a disgusted shrug of his shoulders.

"The brute!" said Jocelyn, her face crimson with sudden anger. "I should like to wring his neck, only"—recovering herself slightly under the surprise in her aunt's and Nielsen's faces, "it looks so dirty."

Giles glanced at her sympathetically—he knew her great love for all birds and animals, and understood.

"You must not be angry with the poor man," said Nielsen, "they are not a sportin' people, the Italians, don't you know."

But Jocelyn's feelings were still ruffled.

"I hate people who drop their final g's," she said.

Nielsen regarded her through his eyeglass with great consternation.

"I beg your pardon," he said at last.

"My *dear*!" said Mrs. Travis—want of affability in *other* people was a crime to her, it rendered things so uncomfortable.

"Oh! You are excused," said Jocelyn, whose sudden anger had evaporated now that they were out of sight of the intending sportsman—"it doesn't matter for foreigners, you know, only you mustn't do it again."

She experienced a sudden compunction, and smiled at him appealingly.

Nielsen, who accepted her shrewdly as one not to be judged by ordinary standards, liked her the better for the swift changing of her moods.

They passed through Ventimiglia and along the level road that runs to Bordighera; past the odorous tannery, past the town's custom-house, past the ill-looking, outlying, roadside cafés.

A villainous Italian, with a dirty face, coming out of one of these, took his slouch hat off to Giles, who returned him a nod.

"Who is that horrid-looking man?" said Jocelyn.

"A friend of mine," replied Giles gravely; "he pays professional visits to the villa sometimes; he is one of a profession the most elevated in these parts, plays the barrel-organ."

"*Ah! Mais ce n'est pas une profession, ça, c'est une carrière vous savez,*" put in Nielsen, sotto voce.

They drove past the long, dull, modern street, and the picturesque town of old Bordighera, tumbled together in lofty and evil-smelling seclusion above. At the garden of palms beyond, the drive came to an end.

Some one suggested picnicking on the rocks below the road; they left the carriage, and made their way down to the beach, where they lunched in the shade of a huge, seaworn boulder.

After the things were cleared and taken back to the carriage, Giles returned from giving directions to the coachman to find Mrs. Travis on the verge of sleep, her mouth slightly open, her hand feebly grasping a drooping parasol, her head nodding from side to side.

He could see Jocelyn at the water's edge, and Nielsen moving towards her; and he felt a great pang of jealousy.

Lighting a cigar, he strolled away from Mrs. Travis; he did not wish to embarrass the good lady upon her awakening. With his hat over his eyes, he leant against a rock, sending vicious puffs of smoke between his lips, and looking down at a footprint Jocelyn had left in the sand.

Chapter Seven

JOCELN had strolled away by herself—she had a longing to be alone with the sea. She did not know exactly what it was that she wanted, but it seemed to her that the sea would give her a feeling of rest. She was annoyed presently to find Nielsen beside her. He had humbly brought her the service of his green-lined umbrella, and she had not the heart to send him away, when he asked gently if he bored her.

They strolled together towards a group of rocks that jutted in a blunt, curving point into the sea.

"I want to get on that little green rock," said Jocelyn, pointing to the furthermost rock separated from the others by an eddy of rippling, shallow water. In a moment she had whipped off her shoes and stockings, and with skirts raised to her ankles, was scrambling through the ripples of the circling waves, up the slippery, green slope of the rock.

Nielsen regarded her proceedings from the beach with an air of comical dismay and admiration.

"Take care, my dear young lady," he kept on saying, rolling his r's more than usual. His eyeglass was damp with the interest of his glance, and his umbrella hung uselessly over his shoulder.

"Come along," said Jocelyn, "I thought you used to be an athlete?"

"It was not the part of the athlete in my day to climb slippery rocks with young ladies," he said plaintively, gallantly removing a boot, and standing on one leg in an amiable hesitation.

"*Mais en verité*," he muttered to himself, drawing off the other boot and revealing pink socks, in the toe of one of which was a decided hole; "she is not a milk and butter Miss, *cette chère* Jocelyn," and he hastily divested himself of the holey sock.

Jocelyn having reached the summit, dropped her skirts, and, shading her face with her hand from the burning sun, looked over the hesitating Nielsen at the lines of the bay, that curved in under the stony, sparsely-covered mountains.

It was one of those cloudless Riviera days, when, seen from behind the sun, the coast loses all other colouring in the vivid tints of the sky and sea. The blue of the distant Esterelles melted in the far west into the paler blue of the heavens, and all the nearer hills and jutting promontories were bathed in a wonderful violet ether. One ultimate snowy peak reared itself aloft, emerging triumphant from the trammels of the light. Looking eastwards, where the sun had already sped his course, every line and patch of colouring was thrown into an intense relief. The white houses stared along the stony, drab slopes. The Campanile with the little black cross upon its summit, sprang up high over the old town of Bordighera, against masses of glistening olives beyond. Along a far spur of the hills an old Italian village stretched in straggling seclusion.

Jocelyn bent over to look into the turquoise pools that lapped with white edges round the green, weed-covered rocks, and now and again caught the shadowy gleam of a fish in the cloudy-blue water. On the next rock to her, two picturesque bare-legged fishers angled lazily with twelve-foot rods of stiff bamboo. The breeze caught her hair, and she turned and looked away over the sea, drawing the soft, salt air through her nostrils with an intense feeling of pleasure.

She was in one of her gipsy moods—it was good to set her back to the land, to those eternal ridges of hills which forced upon her a feeling of imprisonment; very good to turn to the sea, the salt sea, stretching before her in blue, illimitable vastness.

A wonderful glow of life and freedom came upon her with the beating of the soft wind against her face. She felt a wild desire to spread her wings in a long, long flight to a freer life, like the little, lateen-rigged fishing smack, running from the land before the wind—a flight away from convention, and the eternal need for repression; away from all her fears, from the horror which sometimes came over her, from the unconfessed longing which fought against it within her breast; away, into a solitude as great as the sea itself, where no other individualities should besiege her own, giving her a sense of suffocation—a solitude, where there should be no knowledge, and no distrust.

Nielsen's gently imperturbable voice recalled her.

"I am coming, my dear young lady; just a little patience, it is very slipperry, don't you see." He was picking a gingerly way with his bare feet from one stone to another.

"Go back," she cried almost harshly. "I'm coming off!"

What was the use of her wild thoughts! She was bound to that undefined struggle which, whether she would or no, was always going on within her. Her face clouded with its wonted look of defeat, and she sighed. She waited till Nielsen was returning, and then waded back herself.

The feelings which the sea had roused in her made her irritable.

"It's a dull sea—the Mediterranean," she said from one side of a rock, putting on her shoes and stockings, "no tides, no ebb and flow; what a monotony! I wonder it finds it worth while to break on its shores at all!"

"You would not say that if you saw it in a storm," came, in plaintive, half-choked parenthesis, from the other side of the rock, where the discreet Swede was also resuming his boots.

"It manages to break on every shore all round; I should like to know where it parts its hair," continued Jocelyn meditatively.

"My dear young lady, it is like the bald-headed man, don't you know; it does not part its hair at all, it has no hair to part in the middle, don't you see, only a fringe that falls on all sides."

Nielsen appeared suddenly from round the rock, his hat in his hand, smoothing his own well-covered, flaxen head appreciatively.

Jocelyn laughed gently. She had finished her toilet, and sat looking up at him with her head a little on one side, and her feet drawn under her skirts. Nielsen moved a step towards her, and his brown eyes glowed.

"Do you know you are quite charming! May I not—"—he bent his head to her hand.

'Please don't!" she said impatiently.

She had lately found it difficult to take the sentimental remarks of the enamoured Swede as a matter of course.

"Forgive me," said Nielsen humbly, "you are so beautiful, you see!"

"I would rather you didn't talk like that, please," said Jocelyn.

She rose and held out her hand to him frankly; Nielsen took it in his own, letting it go with a deep sigh.

Jocelyn restrained an inclination to laugh.

"What is that ship?" she asked, as they made their way towards the others. Nielsen screwed his eyeglass into his eye.

"A 'messageries' for China and the Indies; she will call at Genoa."

Jocelyn's eyes followed the great, black steamer racing past. The foam was churning up from under its bows, and along its sides. She looked at it wistfully with wide eyes—the longing was not out of her yet. Nielsen fastened on the look intuitively.

"If you would marry me, you should do that or anything else that you liked," he said suddenly, pointing to the steamer; "I am not verry poor now, you know—the 'system' has been verry good to me lately."

There was an earnestness in his voice, that was in strong contrast to its habitual suave flattery, and his allusion to the "system" —which, with a gambler's superstition, he never mentioned— struck Jocelyn. She stopped and looked at him.

Yes! He was evidently in earnest; the innumerable little lines and crow's-feet in his face, showed cruelly in the blazing sunshine; he was paler than usual, and he looked at her with almost a dog's look in his weary brown eyes. But all she said was—

"I think you spend too much time over the 'system'!"

She caught sight of Giles's figure against the rock, and she felt a sudden, physical repulsion to the man standing beside her.

"But understand," said Nielsen, "I love you—I love you! You cannot prevent that, you know." He put out his hands, as if to take her in his arms, and his face twitched.

"Are you mad?" she cried, hurrying past him. She walked swiftly over the hard sand, and as she went a curious feeling came upon her, a feeling of delight that was almost pain. She had forgotten Nielsen, but the words, "I love you—I love you," kept echoing within her; they had lost all sound and form, they had become like the breath of an inspiration. All her being rose in a trembling answer. A wave of crimson rushed into her face, and as she hastened she plucked nervously at the single yellow rose fastened in her dress. Nielsen stood still, looking after her. A minute later, however, he was beside her again, talking commonplaces with his usual plaintive, imperturbable drawl, his face showing no traces of its recent emotion.

When they reached the others, Jocelyn threw herself down by her aunt, close to a group of sea-washed rocks, through the broken crevices of which the little waves were leaping and flashing like white fairies at play; and when Giles came up, two minutes later, she seemed to be listening gaily to a story Nielsen was telling. Mrs. Travis, fanning herself, insinuated gentle complaints of the heat. She wished to see the palm gardens, where it looked shady.

Giles led the way with alacrity; he longed to have Jocelyn to himself, with all the concentrated longing of many hours of repression. Mrs. Travis was soon in rapt admiration of the shrubs and flowers; and she impressed Nielsen into her service to make a bargain in French with the florist proprietor, for a weekly provision of flowers to be sent to Mentone, standing by to afford assistance; she had a great and wholly warranted faith in her powers of cheapening things.

Giles and Jocelyn strolled away from them, and were soon hidden by the thick palm foliage. The garden wound up and down in a mass of flowering plants and scented shrubs.

"It's a kind of paradise," said Giles, "rather cut and dried in parts."

"Yes," Jocelyn assented—" 'the trail of the florist is over it all.' But the scents are good; I love the dear flowers." She plucked a spray of roses daringly, and pinned them in the breast of her dress.

"I was always a thief with flowers, you know; I can't help it, I *have* to steal them."

Presently they followed a little path running upwards at the top of the garden. It led them on to a rocky knoll over which, in a ring of spikey aloes and grotesque prickly pears, a shady olive spread its shimmering branches like a tent. Jocelyn seated herself beneath it, looking down upon the wilderness of the garden foliage. In her white skirt and pale silver-green blouse, she looked like the spirit of the tree, as she leant against the trunk with the yellow sunlight playing fantastically on her through the quivering leaves.

A bare and stony hill sloped behind them, planted here and there with vines and rose-trees, which served only to throw into a greater relief its yellow-grey harshness. In front, the tangled masses of palms and plants, the plain, unpretentious white houses straggling along the shore, and the straight line of the railway running beside the sea, gave the scene the unfinished look of some sub-tropical settlement. Across the dipped valley, under the lee of a high, rounded hill covered with olives and glancing green fig-trees, a little church spire rose modestly and incongruously out of a mass of palms.

Giles, who had turned the brim of his Panama hat down, like a mushroom, over his neck, lay on his face in the sun, looking up at Jocelyn. Her beauty, and the impelling, passionate yearning within him, deprived him helplessly of the power of speech. She was sitting with her hand on Shikari's head, smelling at the flowers in her dress, her figure swaying a little as she hummed to herself. Her cheeks were still flushed, and her eyes bright from that strange emotion.

She began to sing a little Finnish song, that he knew well, with notes that suggested "sobbing" for a refrain. She had a tiny voice, "*niedlich*," as the Germans say. But in the middle of a verse she stopped suddenly and pointed with her ungloved hand at a large, yellow-fanged drover's dog, which had appeared on the side of the knoll. Shikari sprang up with a growl, his teeth showing. The two dogs approached one another snarling, and before Giles could rise to prevent them, had each other by the throat, and were rolling over and over on the ground. He leaped hastily to his feet, and gripped Shikari hard by the collar, getting a purchase with his foot against the other dog's shoulder, with a violent, pushing kick, he sent him sprawling down the slope.

As he turned his head for a second, he saw Jocelyn holding Shikari with her arms laced round his neck—the dog was growling and licking her face at the same time—but in another minute the drover's dog came up the slope again, and with a savage snarl, sprang at his throat.

Throwing out both hands stiffly, he caught at the brute's neck, but his grip slipped on the short, wiry hair, and the impetus of the dog's spring carried him backwards on to the ground.

Jocelyn saw his hands slip, saw him stagger, and fall; it seemed impossible to her that he could keep those hideous fangs from his throat. Involuntarily she threw her hands up to her eyes. She had a mental vision of a torn throat—a gaping, jagged wound. A cloud of hot, whirling dust rose from the dry ground, where the man and beast were struggling. For one second of sheer horror she stood still, her face crimson and as suddenly white, then with a little cry she ran towards them; but the struggle was already over. The first movement of her hands had released the greyhound. The drover's dog had turned with his teeth on Giles's throat to attack his old enemy, and Giles scrambling to his feet, had seized his stick, dealing the brute a heavy blow, which half stunned him.

Jocelyn saw him leaning over the two dogs, a hand twisted in the collar of each, his face very pale, his figure strained with the effort of holding them apart; his clothes were covered with dust, and he bled from a scratch on one hand. He released the cowed brute, who slunk away down the hill, and stood up, breathing hard, keeping a foot on Shikari, who growled angrily.

Jocelyn went softly up to him. Even now, seeing him erect, she hardly dared look at his throat, so vivid was the memory of the wound that had gleamed, red and angry, before her covered eyes.

She gave a little choke and put out her hands.

When he felt the touch of her fingers on his shoulder he faced her suddenly. In the moments of fierce excitement, when his muscles and his nerves had been strung and braced, all thought of Jocelyn had left him, he had felt only the fighting fever and the consciousness of strength; but his blood was coursing wildly through his veins, and the touch of those fingers was like a spark to a magazine. All his passion returned with tenfold strength.

He faced her with blazing eyes, and his lips quivered.

"Are you hurt, Giles?" she said.

Her eyes were bent on him with a strained look, the black pupils expanding; and her lips were tremulous and parted.

'My darling!" he cried, "did you care?"

She looked at him, frightened at his words, yet wondering he should ask.

"Care? Yes."

"I love you, Jocelyn, I love you! My God! What am I saying?"

He bent his head down to the level of her hands; one of them stole up and smoothed his hair with a little shrinking caress.

When he looked again, her eyes were soft and wet, and he knew somehow that she had been glad.

He was nearly choked by the joy that leaped in his heart, but the tears in her eyes helped him to a mastery of himself.

"Dear," he said, "I am sorry, I couldn't help it! Forget it—forgive me, I couldn't help it—you are so sweet and lovely—so sweet and lovely—after all, you knew it long ago."

He spoke in short, broken sentences, catching his breath with gasps.

She smiled at him softly and sadly, and for one moment he caught, as in a revelation, the love-light in her eyes. Her lips still trembled; with her hands she brushed the dust mechanically from his clothes.

She looked swiftly up at him.

"I was so frightened," she said, "I thought—" and covered her eyes with her hands, shuddering.

He caught them in his, and stood looking down upon her dark head. He could see the little fluffy hair on her neck, and her shoulders heaving softly. He was too happy to speak; and he was afraid—afraid of the passionate words that rose to his lips. The dry leaves of the olive tree rustled crisply over their heads, and from the road below came the tinkle of cowbells.

Voices broke in upon their silence. They went down in answer to Mrs. Travis's calling, and as they went, Giles said softly—

"Whatever comes, dear, this has been the hour of my life."

They drove home without stopping at the villa, putting Nielsen down at the Ventimiglia station. He had been very silent on the return journey. He said to Jocelyn when he left them—

"I must get back to Monte Carlo, you know, and appease the Fates for my desertion."

As they passed the last hill into Mentone the evening light was already spreading, mellow and soft, over the town, and the sun was dying behind the Esterelles. The tired little horses, toiling up the steep ascent, nodded their heads diligently.

Jocelyn and Giles got out to walk. Half-way up, Jocelyn stopped and stretched out her arms, saying with a sigh—

"Look! The evening is coming over everything, like a cool blessing, gentle—gentle—"

"Yes!" said Giles. Their eyes met for one moment, and not another word was said.

When they reached the hotel, he took his leave of them. Jocelyn turned on the steps.

"*Buona Sera!* my friend!" she said. " *Buona Sera!*" She gave him her hand for a second time. Her eyes looked unnaturally large in the uncertain light. Giles stood with his hat off till she had disappeared—he could not speak.

Chapter Eight

THE sun sank, leaving a pale glory of silver-green light over the clear-cut edges of the mountain range. Masses of heavy, purple clouds threatened the silver halo, and in the remote west, a smoky, yellow flare lingered over the Esterelles. One little star trembled like a pure spirit above the highest peaks, and under the Tête du Chien the closely coiled ring of lights at Monte Carlo twinkled through the growing darkness.

Far away, up an inland valley, a single splash of crimson light showed where some chance fire raged unchecked among the mountain forest-growth. Through the perfume of orange trees a floating smoke-wrack of burning wood spent itself upon the warm air. The air was full too of early evening sounds—the barking of dogs, the crack of a whip lash, the hardly-caught metallic murmur of human voices, the rattle of a receding train, and over all the croaking of the frogs, and the sighing of the sea.

Giles swung along the road on his way back to the villa like a man in a dream.

"*Buona Sera!—buona Sera!*"—the words rang in his ears. The blood was coursing through his veins, and his pulses beat wildly. For the time he was no longer conscious of that ever haunting thought, "What the devil was he doing in that galley?" He let himself go on the flood tide of his passion. Jocelyn's image danced along the road in front of him. He saw her pale face, under her shady hat, looking at him with soft, dark eyes, through the dim shadows of every road-side tree.

He had walked, like a man possessed, up the long hill to the Pont St. Louis. The gendarmes whom he passed at the Customs looked after him curiously.

"*Buona Sera!* There is one who marches, hein! Diable enragé d'un Anglais. *Peste!* he has not stopped for the gambler's leap. *Buona Sera, signore!*" In the alternative they decided that he had broken the bank.

"*Buona Sera!*" Over the bridge, with its sheer descent to the dim caves on the one side, and the twinkling cottage lights on the other, and up and still up the hill. He could smell the perfume of her dress in every evening scent, in the salt whiffs wafted from below, in the fragrance of the lonely pine trees above the road.

"*Buona \Sera! Buona Sera!*" The words were in the distant croaking of the frogs, on every murmur of the breaking waves.

As he drew his breath freely again after the steep ascent, he looked far out over the cliffs, to the westward, in the still evening light, and his thoughts flew to the girl as she had stood on the hotel steps waving her hand to him. How he loved the delicate, dainty figure, the turn of the slender neck, the pure line of her profile, the softly pointed chin! He pictured her as she had sat under the olive in the afternoon, looking up at the sky through the delicate tracery of its leaves—the creamy white line of the pretty throat bent back, the long, supple hands lying in her lap. He felt an intense, unreasoning delight that, for good or evil, he had told her of his love; then an infinite, tender compassion for her tremulous silence, for the little, swaying, helpless motion of her head and hands, for the swift, dewy glance of her dark eyes.

She *knew*—nothing could take that from him; she *knew*, and she had been glad to know.

Now that the keynote had been struck, all the deep chords, unstirred for so many years in his mind, sounded with a full consonance; all the great, unsatisfied longing hitherto unshadowed in his deeply affectionate nature had taken to itself shape, all the vast gambling possibility in him was fiercely aroused.

The latent force, the unspent passion of the years that he had idled away, shallow and indifferent, in a long, unbroken compromise with life, asserted themselves now with a fatal vehemence. He was not a man who could love without passion. Passion would play its full part in his love, neither more nor less; and he knew it.

In the changes that his mind rang on the situation, and the

bewildered jangling of his thoughts, the idea of recoil was the only one that did not come to him. He would go forward, at what cost he did not know, he did not stop to count. He hugged to himself, undiscerning of what it meant, the defeat of the eternal compromise.

Again he moved homewards, now idling slowly along, and her words, "The evening is coming over everything, like a cool blessing, gentle—gentle," sounded in his ears, and he could see again her arms outstretched as though to take it to herself.

He came presently through the scented night to the villa, and let himself in with a sudden, chill feeling of utter languor. He flung himself into a long chair in the unlighted drawing-room, and, worn out, fell fast asleep.

To Irma, as she raised the curtains that divided the room from her own boudoir, there was the look of a wrecked man about him as he lay there. The long figure was thrown carelessly down in its dusty, white clothes, the neck bent slightly back, and the head rested on an arm twisted behind him. A bar of yellow light from the half-shaded lamp she held in her hand fell across his lean, sun-tanned face and neck, sharpening the features, and throwing into relief the lines which seam a man's face when sleep follows on the fiercer emotions. She set the lamp upon a table, and stood, leaning painfully against the wall, thinking.

Her husband! those two words were the epitome of her thoughts. She bent forward, and gazed at him long and closely, as if she had never seen him before. How tired he looked! After all, it was the face of a stranger!—ten years of married life, and the face of a stranger! She smiled, a very weary smile. A fine face, with a good brow and chin, now that it was rid of the mask it had worn to her these ten years! She read in its lines things she had never known were there, and *another* woman had brought them into the face! *That* was the mischief of it! and the pain! She passed her thin hand across her eyes with a sudden, swift gesture. In her own mind, too, she was finding things she had not suspected. She had thought it impossible she should ever feel *that* pain, that sudden jealous spasm.

She stood quite motionless, a bent figure, thinking. The day of her wedding came back to her, a day of indifferent obedience to her parents. All the long vista of days since rose before her mind— a level, monotonous line of ghosts.

Her lips trembled as if with cold; she muttered to herself in Polish, "I have no claim upon him." What was it to her that he should go from her? what had it ever been? Go from her! when he had never been hers. And yet—a vision of Jocelyn, as she had stood that morning, smiling and graceful, talking to the birds, rose before her. A blind, wearing pain of jealous regret was come to torture her. She thought, "It is hard!"

She moved, with one hand on her breast, to the window and stood, looking out into the soft, hazy night. The shadow of her drooping, white-robed figure fell across the bar of light from the flaring lamp.

Yes! he had been very good to her, very good and gentle—few men, she thought, would have been so gentle to a helpless log, such as she had always been. And what had she given him in return? And now—too late! Well, it was natural, this which was happening, only she wished—bitterly, fiercely, vainly wished—that it had not come. She felt tired, and very far spent; he would not have had to wait long!

A faint stir of air ruffled the lace round her thin throat; a whisper behind her said, "Jocelyn!"

She turned to see Giles sitting up, with one hand stretched out, and rubbing his eyes with the other; as she turned he woke to his full consciousness, and a low "Ah, you!" escaped from his lips.

Again a choking spasm of jealousy came upon her, again a vision of the girl passed before her eyes, but she held the quiver out of her voice.

"It does not matter," she said, but her eyes, black and mournful, looked wild in the dim, smoky light.

Giles put his hands before his face, and bent forward in his chair.

"I am sorry," was all he said.

Irma turned from the window, and straightened her drooping figure. She took the lamp in her hand, and moved to the door.

"Good night, Giles! It does not matter, there is nothing to be done, you know—nothing."

The voice sounded staccato, level, monotonous, as if the words were ground out of her; only her eyes, in the backward look she gave him, had meaning.

And from the bent figure, in the darkness of the room behind her, came a muttered word—"Nothing."

Chapter Nine

In her bedroom Jocelyn was thinking. The inner door stood open, and from the next room came a stream of murmured comments, broken now and then by a mumble, denoting pins in the mouth, or by the trickle of water into a basin. Mrs. Travis was going to bed; she loved to relieve the monotony of the process by discussion upon the events of the day, which never assumed such vast proportions as when she was taking her leave of them.

Jocelyn leant, in her night-dress, against her open window, smoking a tiny cigarette through a long amber mouthpiece. She drew at the cigarette, and, holding it far from her, puffed vigorously through her parted lips; the smoke, caught by the faint out-draught, blew harmlessly away in little wreaths and clouds.

Her aunt's voice came to her in jerky, complacent periods.

"How hot the nights are getting! We can't stay here much longer, my dear, nobody stays till June, it's very late already. If it wasn't for my new 'system', I wouldn't stay another day—I'm sure there's something in it." She appeared for a moment at the door with her arms raised rectangularly to her back hair.

"How thin Giles is growing!" she said in an injured voice, with a shrewd look at her niece. "It makes me quite uncomfortable to see him."

It was a canon with her that people should be plump. She was alive to the state of Giles's feelings, but she resented its affecting the outlines of his person. From much experience she felt secure of her niece's invulnerability, she had seen so many darts fall blunted from her armour, one adorer more or less, even a married one, did not matter. She always reflected, too, that Giles was a connection of her own by marriage. Mrs. Travis possessed that order of mind which looks upon things belonging to themselves as beyond suspicion and reproach. He was a married man, but a connection of her own, immaculate! Nevertheless she resented the dwindling of his bulk; perhaps she considered it indecent; perhaps, in some mysterious way, she regarded it as the removal of her own property. In any case a moody leanness was unpardonable; to her, Nielsen, attentive yet well-covered, was more satisfactory.

"I shall recommend him to take cod-liver oil; I don't think it's right for any man to be so thin," she said.

Jocelyn made an impatient movement, and the frilled sleeves of her night-dress rustled faintly against the muslin curtain. Mrs. Travis, disappearing again into her room, continued to talk.

"To-day was quite wasted; we mustn't gad about so much; I ought to have been at the tables. Yes, I shall stay the month out, but the first of June we must go; remind me to take the roses off my new bonnet." Her voice, overpowered by pins, ran into a mumble.

Jocelyn braced her slender, curving limbs against the wall. "Go!" The word brought her an unpleasant shock of reminder. She threw up her head impatiently. Her small, oval face looked very childish and young in the loose framework of dark hair, brushed in long, rippling tresses back over her shoulders. In the darkened room her slight figure, in its thin white covering, was dimly outlined, and the bare feet, thrust forward as she leaned back, gleamed in a little patch of light that came from the other room.

Mrs. Travis came to the door. She was more comfortable than ever in her night attire, with a comfort that threw off all attempts at decorative disguise, solely excepting curl papers.

"You naughty girl, you're smoking!" she said.

Jocelyn shrugged her shoulders.

"It's for the mosquitoes, and the nerves."

"Well, I don't like it—my dear mother would have had convulsions if she'd seen you. I don't think it's right! Shut your windows, and keep the mosquitoes out, as I do." She sniffed.

Jocelyn gave a prolonged puff, and flipped the cigarette out of its holder.

"There!" she said. "Run, or the beasts will eat you, you are so good to them."

Mrs. Travis, with a hasty kiss, retreated rapidly, closing the door. Jocelyn laughed, then she moved restlessly up and down the room. Presently she came back to the window, and leaned far out into the darkness. It was late; the town slept, vaguely stretched below in a rambling confusion of dark shapes and corners, foliage, and dimly burning lights. It was very still. . . .

In the girl's heart joy and pain were strangely blended.

The first of June! This was the seventh of May, nearly a month, that was all! What did it mean? Whither was she being carried? If it could only be always as it had been that evening! She had been so happy. In less than a month she would go away! It seemed very strange, very unreal; there was a desperate discomfort in the thought, the discomfort of unfulfilment.

The vague, dreaming sweetness was being rudely rent away from her thoughts—the glamour that hung like a veil over the past day. For a moment she saw plainly all the naked, unsparing reality. She heard again the words of the sick woman, "Have a good time, you are young, you are beautiful—it is fitting." The devilish, unconscious irony of them! She felt a great sense of injustice, of hard usage at the hands of fate.

That day a wonderful sweetness had come to her. It was as if, for the first time, life had whispered some secret of hidden meaning, had spoken words at which the longing and the lonely restlessness of her soul had yielded. This was love! Love!

She laughed. The mockery and hopelessness of it were so plain that she felt its strength the more. Her eyes moved restlessly from side to side as if seeking a way of escape—she twisted her hands silently, and pressed them to her cheek. She loved him, and he was beyond her reach—why? why? She chafed under the thought.

The passionate, penetrating cry of a peacock broke suddenly through the vibrating air; it echoed painfully within her. Why should she not know love? What had she done? She had not sought —could she help it? Why put it away? It was sweet and good to be with him, she wanted nothing more. Then there flashed before her the look in Giles's eyes, as he gazed at her after his struggle with the dog; for one most disquieting moment she saw into them, behind them; he knew there *was* something further, beyond, some-

67

thing fundamental, burning, unknown to her, which passed by, scorching her like a fiery breath. And for that moment she shrank back frightened, ashamed, and thrust the shutters to, to drive out the long, fiercely wailing regret in the shrill, bird's cry.

The figure of the Polish woman, lying in its white drapery, came before her. A woman with haunting, unhappy eyes, ill—her friend, his wife—her friend! She made a little impatient movement in the dark room, and groping, turned to her bed with a shrinking desire to hide herself. She felt as if in the presence of something contaminating and poisonous; she shuddered, her pride revolted. She drew aside the curtains, and flung herself upon the bed. What had she done? Why should she be treated like this? Tears of impotent rage and self-pity filled her eyes. It was all so new, so strange, so unreal. She drew the clothes over her, as a child does to drive away the fear of bogies. She would not think of these things; there seemed a safety and a refuge in the soft pillows and the familiar cool rustle of the sheets as she turned from side to side. She lay a long time rigid, trying not to think, vaguely uneasy, vaguely unhappy, vaguely frightened; she was tired too. But in spite of herself all the mingled feelings of the past weeks came back to her. The rude shock, so long ago now, of awakening to the knowledge that he loved her—the horror of it; that horror, which was but sharpened by the something in her own heart which she would not confess. All the weary struggle and repression for days and days with no certain knowledge of what she desired. And this was the end! He could never be hers—and she loved him! She buried her face in the pillows, and sobbed as if her heart would break.

After a long time, she fell into a half-conscious, restless state. Motionless and unreasoning, she passed in succession through all the events of the day gigantically exaggerated, blending grotesquely one into the other; then through each one of them, startlingly distinct, having no relation to any other thing that had ever happened to her—visions of things, which seemed like vast shadow-throwing rocks one might encounter in a desert of sand. Then again, in sudden change, a great, blurred mist of vaporous phantoms came before her. One by one she strove to attain them—they were without form and void, and one by one they passed her by, remote and mournful as the flight of a lapwing. Images, carved in the air, of people she had known, of faces she had never seen; words she had heard, words that had never been spoken, flitted by, hovering like moths with restless wings. All that she had ever done, seen, or heard, was before her in a dancing maze of coloured shapes, threading singly to the centre of a blazing wheel, darting outwards radiant to the misty circle edge, like flight of gnats round a fire. The lids fast-closed over her eyes seemed to enclose the world for her, to drive down into her brain a mass of wheeling unreality. With an effort she wrenched herself free from her pillows, tossing her bare arms over her head. She fell back again, with one hand clasped behind her thick, soft hair, looking up with wide eyes at the dim shape of the curtained bed roof. It was thus that sleep presently found her. . . .

When she awoke in the morning, a faint feeling of frightened discomfort, a feeling that something new and dangerous was before her, vanished with the slanting, brilliant beams of sun striking through the shutters. She lay, quietly twisting a wisp of her tumbled hair, surprised only that she had forgotten to plait it the night before. Then, as everything came back to her with a rush, she wondered what she had found to so trouble and alarm her. Giles loved her!—well, it was very sweet and good to be loved by him, and she could not help it. She only wanted to be with him— to know that he loved her! What harm was there! She sprang from the bed.

The pulse of life beat very strongly this morning in the green-clothed, quivering valley behind the town; the almond trees seemed to flush a deeper pink; the tinkle of bells, as goats shifted dustily along the road to a new pasture, came with fuller melody to her ears. She leaned from the window and drew in a deep breath of the freshened air.

After all, there was nearly a month, and life was good just now —nearly a month of a sweet companionship, and after—well—all things come to a end!—it was not very good to dwell upon that thought, it was better to take things as they came. She fell to wondering what time Giles would be with them.

That morning Mrs. Travis, in pursuance of her resolve, went early into Monte Carlo. She knew that Giles would come over, but she always shut her eyes to the possibility of mischief, knowing that to recognise it would mean the sacrifice of her daily visit to the gambling-tables. Taking the greatest care never to dive below the surface, she was enabled to persuade herself quite comfortably that her niece ran no risk, and she consoled herself for leaving her with her habitual reflection that Giles was a connection of her own— the elasticity of her principles enabling her that morning to fix the relationship at some two degrees nearer than it really was. He was also a married man, a fact which she could twist either way as it suited her convenience, with an equally full and just feeling of comfort. She departed, getting over the ground at a great pace with a dignified, flat-footed gait, her head full of enthusiasm and artificial flowers. She studied, as she went, a little book on her "system" —without in the least understanding it, which was immaterial, as she always abandoned it after playing it for a quarter of an hour. She assured Jocelyn comfortably, on parting from her, that she would be back quite early, and Jocelyn looked after her, smiling, perfectly assured that she would be free till dinner.

Giles came soon after; his face, impassively haggard, lighted up when Jocelyn came towards him. She had never seemed to him so beautiful and full of life. She gave him both her hands, with the intuitive feeling that in frank friendliness alone lay a narrow path of safety and happiness for the days left to them. She looked at him softly, and so took from him the bitterness which might have driven him to passionate words. In the reaction of a long, sleepless night he had schooled himself painfully to accept this position, but he was relieved beyond measure not to have to take the initiative. It hurt him to see those two hands so frankly stretched to him, but he was grateful to her, with a dull, despairing sort of gratitude.

He had not seen his wife since the scene of the night before— the impression left upon him by it was too strong and painful. For the space of a short hour, he had proposed to himself not to see Jocelyn again, to keep away at all costs, but his resolve had shrivelled, like all his resolves, before the flame of his passion, and he had come, with the reservation to let yesterday's words be as if unspoken.

He spent the whole day with her, and went home in the evening humble, and almost happy. He was worn out by the conflicting emotions of the previous day and his sleepless night. . . .

A fortnight of days went by, and as the sands of their hour-glass of time ran out, the strain upon them became almost unbearable. Jocelyn's continual thought was, "I shall go away, and there will be the end!" But she found that there were moments when she was dumb with the dull craving to feel his arms round her. At other times she longed to get away at once, anywhere away; to be free for ever, and at all costs, from this grinding necessity for repression, from the appealing, haunting look which Giles could not keep out of his face. With the constant varying of her moods their meetings became daily more difficult, the hours spent together more feverish or more dismal. Once Giles broke through the intolerable restraint, but the piteous, frightened look that came into her face at the first word held him mute.

Never for one moment did Jocelyn doubt herself. She would go away, and there would be the end! But the very impossibility of union with him, which she kept ever before her as the one barrier of safety, roused at times in her feelings before which she recoiled ashamed, which she had never thought that her mind could harbour—curiosity to probe her lover's nature to its depths, ardent longing to know, and to prove the full meaning of the passion she saw in his eyes, felt in every touch of his fingers. At other times she had an intense, passionless pity for the suffering he could not hide from her. And sometimes the old horror came over her, and she would turn from him with aversion, only to be smitten with remorse when he had left her.

She had no one to help her in her trouble; the thought of confiding in her aunt never even occurred to her, so completely was that lady associated with the conventional crust of life.

In these days Giles lived only in the minutes that he was with her; the knowledge that she loved him served but to fan the flame of his passion. Often after he had left her, he would come back when it was dark, and, standing in the shadow of the thick bushes along the terrace wall, watch her bedroom window till the light within it failed.

One night he had watched long; the light behind the closed shutters still sent a faint glow into the soft darkness. Leaning against the wall he waited for it to die. A bat flitted past; great moths fluttered out of the night towards the lamps at the gates; dull murmurs came from the street, and always the frogs croaked. The scented laurel behind which he stood gave forth a sweet, hot odour. Suddenly the shutters of the window swung back, and in the arch of light he saw Jocelyn. She stood motionless, with her hands clasped behind her head; the sleeves of the loose, white garment wrapped around her fell back from her bare arms.

His heart stopped beating; the breath of the laurel was heavy in the air, and ever afterwards its scent brought back with it the sweetness and emotion of that memory.

As she stood, with her face lifted to the purple heaven where the pale stars gleamed fitfully, he could see the masses of her dark hair hanging loose upon her shoulders. He felt, as though with the yearning of his gaze through the impassive darkness, his whole being clung to her in a mute caress, as though her heart were beating against him, her lips quivering upon his own; and, as if in answer, her hands fell to her sides, and she leant forward on the balcony, looking downwards. Breathless he watched. With a swift movement she clasped her hands together into the darkness, and then pressed them to her forehead. Through the sudden hush of the night he could hear her weeping; his passion swelled in one long, dumb cry, and ebbed in a sob of pity. With her face still buried in her hands, she turned inwards with a swaying movement. The shutters swung slowly to, and the light died. . . .

A cockchafer droned by him, its hum fading into the night. With a groan he beat his fists against the wall.

Chapter Ten

Two figures came slowly down the hill from the heights of Belinda to the Pont St. Louis. Darkness was closing in upon them. In front, vanishing in the dusk along the white road, their donkeys, relieved of burden, jingled homewards at an irregular gait. The girl driver, her wide, conical Mentonese hat hanging over her arm, and a flower in her mouth, flicked their lean haunches with her whip. She walked, fast and erect, with a swaying of her hips, exchanging rough jests with the Gendarmes at the Customs. The basket she carried in her hand swung gently with a subdued rattle of empty bottles and plates.

Giles stopped on the bridge. He put his hand on Jocelyn's arm, and the touch of his fingers was hot upon her flesh through her light muslin sleeve.

"There is no hurry," he said in constrained tones which seemed to pass through rigid lips, "it will be over soon enough; let the beasts get on, they make too much noise."

Jocelyn stopped too, looking anxiously into his face; it was set and hard. He leant against the parapet of the bridge, and his profile showed clear-cut through the dusk. One hand gripped the stone coping; she put her own gently upon it. His tall figure quivered from head to foot at the touch, but he kept his eyes away from her face. Presently he began to speak in a measured, expressionless voice.

"Nice place for the end of things, isn't it?" he said, pointing down the precipitous drop to the dim rocks below. "I've known

73

three fellows who ended there—very good chaps; one wouldn't choose it oneself, it can't be pretty;" and he laughed shortly.

"*Don't*, dear!" said Jocelyn, and her hand tightened on his.

His face worked, and he turned to her.

"*Please* take your hand away!"

She drew it away quickly, trembling.

"My God!" he said. "Are you made of ice, Jocelyn? Don't you know what I endure by day and night? Don't you know what a man's love is—Great Heaven! how should you? You *can't* know how it tears and tortures me—" he broke off.

Each word seemed torn from him, and each had a separate, intense value in the still air. He looked down again at the shadowy rocks, then he said—

"I am sorry—there—has—been—a big—mistake—I'm not man enough; come, dear, let's go on."

They moved silently down the deserted road a long way. The growing darkness hid their features from each other. Now they passed through a thick grove of olives that stretched below the road, in banks, to the top of the cliff.

Giles stopped.

"Look!" he said. On the far horizon of the dark sea there was a crimson flare, as of a ship on fire.

"The moon is rising. Sit down a minute, child, and rest, you must be tired."

She seated herself on a lower bank. The moon rose slowly, the crimson changing to yellow, the yellow to white. Giles stood beside the girl, looking down on her. The wonderful southern night throbbed around them, the still air was warm and full of scent; through the olive branches the stars gleamed, there was no sound save the faint, far-off murmur of the town, and the sough of the sea below.

The moon rose to the level of the olive bank; and Giles saw that she was crying, crying silently, pitifully.

He flung himself down at her feet, and kissed them, crying—

"Don't, my darling, don't! it hurts me—it hurts me."

He clasped his hands on her knees, and she bent her head down upon them. A great trembling passed through his frame; it seemed to him an eternity that passed, while the hot moisture of her tears burned his hands. His face was close to her hair; with every

74

noiseless sob it was the nearer to his lips. He kissed the dark head softly.

Presently she raised her eyes to his, dark and wet with tears. Her lips were trembling. The moonbeams fell upon his face, white, tense, and passionate; on hers, tender, pitiful, and tear-stained.

"I *want* to be good to you, dearest. What does anything matter while you are so wretched? What can I do? What can I do?"

He sprang to his feet, and reeled backwards.

"Don't torture me, my darling! You don't know what you're saying," he said in a hoarse whisper, then very deliberately and aloud, "You must go home—go on alone for a minute, I'll come." The words sounded hollow in his own ears, he had a feeling that some one else, not himself at all, had said them. He put his hands over his eyes and muttered indistinctly, "God help me!" with a short choking gasp.

The perfume of her dress and hair was wafted to him, mingled with the night scents, in the intoxicating stillness under those dark branches; he reeled a little, then he saw that Jocelyn too was on her feet. She stood before him quite close, her figure swaying, her breast heaving. In her eyes was an infinite pity; they fastened on his, intent and searching, they seemed trying to read his soul. She put out her hands. He moved with a writhing, helpless gesture, and seized them in his own. With the touch of those burning hands, with the fastening of his eyes on hers, there came a change in the girl's face, the strained look went out of her eyes, they seemed to swim and burn; no longer questioning, they gave him back look for look. Her lips parted slightly in a sigh.

"Sweetheart!" She leaned towards him.

In that second, with his lips almost touching hers, knowing that if they touched there could be no holding back and no recall, everything passed before him. He saw himself. He saw what he was doing. Like a drowning man he saw all that had gone before, all that was coming, stretched grimly into a dim future. He saw her mind—the pity in it, the reflection of his own passion. He saw his wife. He saw *all* things—love, pity, and honour. He weighed them in the scales, they were all as nothing.

A short, sobbing breath of wind sighed through the olives.

Their lips met.

Part II

Chapter Eleven

NIELSEN sat at one of many little marble-topped tables outside a café. It was dark, and the lights of the street avenue shone dubiously on either side through the foliage of the lime trees. From the interior of the café, at his back, the dull clack of dominoes and the flap of waiters' slippered feet against the boarded floor came gently to his ears, with the occasional sharper sounds of men's voices. Through the widely-opened doors and windows stray whiffs of rough, black tobacco, and of garlic, made their way to his nose. The thin strains of harp and mandolin quavered drawlingly into the warm air from a *cantina* lower down the street, and frogs croaked hoarsely in chorus from the bed of the dried watercourse under the bridge.

Nielsen sipped his coffee, smoking quietly. He leant slightly forward, with his shoulders squared, his knees apart, and the rim of his hat pulled forward on his high forehead.

The café was nearly opposite the Hôtel Milano, which stood back from the road in its own garden. Nielsen watched the windows of the hotel, and the vague silhouettes of people's figures against the lighted verandah. The lines of his pale, squarely-moulded face expressed a gently weary resignation, and he remained undisturbed by the wheeling of mosquitoes and the perpetual futile appearances of the unkempt Italian waiters.

That afternoon he had seen Jocelyn for the first time since the day at Bordighera. On that occasion he had been in earnest, with an earnestness that, upon reflection, had caused him surprise. He was aware that he would repeat his conduct under similar circumstances, that the idea of marriage had become so foreign to him in the course of his broken existence, that he was compelled to look upon himself as having deviated from the path of sanity. He had, moreover, been making love to women, more or less harmlessly, for so long, that an acquired cynicism informed him that these things were all a matter of degree, the end of the affair requiring a greater or less absence of the object of attraction. Man of the world, he acutely recognised that without a sustained and zealous siege he had no chance with Jocelyn; he salved his vanity by thinking that, with it, success was possible—even probable. In this way rebuff lost its sting, painful exertion became unnecessary.

The girl had a great attraction for him. She was always "in the picture," her graceful personality was never marred by her surroundings. She had no taint of "insularity." Without self-sufficiency, she seemed sufficient unto herself. All this appealed to the cosmopolitan in him. It was not too much to say, that she more nearly approached the *persona grata* of his fastidious imagination than any woman he had ever met. She was therefore dangerous, he reflected in her absence—in her presence he did not reflect at all, want of reflection in the presence of women having become habitual to him. At this particular moment he was profoundly puzzled.

He had found Jocelyn singularly absorbed, silent and unresponsive. She pleaded headache. Certainly she looked ill, but he had a disquieting feeling that there was something on her mind. She had sat dumb while he talked with her aunt, detailing gossip of the inner life of Monte Carlo, which the soul of that lady loved. When he spoke to her, she was *distraite*, and returned monosyllabic answers. He was not vain enough to attribute her manifest discomfort to his own presence, and, for the first time since he had known her, he came away without feeling the power of her attraction, experiencing instead a sensation of uneasiness and of curiosity, that was purely benevolent and very characteristic.

He had dined at the café, and sat in the dusk waiting till the time for his return train.

A man walking hurriedly on the other side of the street went up through the gates of the hotel garden. Nielsen followed the figure negligently with his eyes, and saw it pass and repass the end of the verandah, and then stand motionless for a long time in the shadow of a tree. The faint inquisitiveness he felt in his movements died away presently in the countless, inconsequent reflections of one not compelled by circumstances to think steadily of any given thing. He yawned, looking at his watch, and throwing away his cigarette stepped out of the circle of light into the road leading to the railway station. As he did so, the man came suddenly down the garden path at a great pace, gesticulating with his clenched hands, passed close without seeing him, and hurried away in the direction of the town, muttering to himself. Nielsen stopped abruptly in recognition. He called after him—

"Hallo! Legard!" The man turned.

"Ah!" he said, "Good night!"

His face was momentarily in the full flare of the café lights; the hat was slouched over it, but the line of his moustache was visible, black against the lower part. The movement of turning had seemed mechanical, the words sounded leaden. In another moment he was gone, walking faster than before, his shoulders hunched up to his ears in a way that suggested pain, and his hands thrust suddenly deep into his pockets as if to keep them still.

Nielsen stood looking after him.

"When a man talks to himself aloud, it is bad!" he said to himself. "When he talks, and clenches his hands *comme ça*, ah! that is very bad! That man is suffering!" He shrugged his shoulders, pointing mechanically with his stick after the figure.

"Yes, yes—I know. I do not like him, but I am sorry for him— he suffers very greatly." He shook his head gravely, as he turned into the station.

.   °   °   ʂ   °

That supreme point, when for a time human nature recoils before suffering in a great lassitude, had not been reached by Giles Legard. Four days of torture had left him still capable of feeling.

Into his bedroom in the little grey villa the moon struck keenly and coldly; there was no other light. He had thrown off coat and waistcoat, and sat motionless, with his head bent on his arms folded across the back of his chair. Upon the table in front of him was a torn envelope and a half sheet of paper, folded and refolded with innumerable creases. The room was empty of all other furniture except the bed, beside which, on a great rug of deerskin stretched over the bare panelling of the floor, Shikari lay, his head between his paws. In the bright moonlight all colours in the room gave way in a harsh contrasting of black and white, and outside the sea gleamed through the tops of the ghostly olives in silver ridges. Every now and then a loosened tendril of creeper swayed with the breath of a newly-born sea wind across the widely-opened casement. From his wife's bedroom underneath came an occasional sound of hollow coughing.

Legard sat with his back turned to the window. The moonlight over the sea brought to him an agonising spasm of memory. . . . In return for an hour of mad, intoxicating passion, he had bartered everything! He took up the sheet of paper, looking at it dully as he twisted it in his hands. He had bartered everything! The thought was old, it seemed to him centuries since he had first realised it. Everything! There was not a shred left to him of his honour, or his self-respect; that did not seem to matter, he was beyond feeling it. But in that single hour of madness he had taken the happiness of the woman he loved—and with it his own—taken it, as it were, in his two hands, and flung it into the dust. Taken her well-being, her reserve, and her pride, and flung them brutally into the dust.

He read the letter mechanically again and again.

"I have tried, but I cannot see you. When you came near everything seemed to cry out at me. It is better that you should keep away—for you and for me. I cannot answer for myself." That was all. No hope! No single stroke of the pen brought relief to his aching spirit.

He held the sheet of paper to catch the full of the moonlight; and her face rose above it, as he had seen it the one time since that night—a delicate, oval face, cold as the moonlight itself; averted and unseizable eyes, profound and dark, with the lids drooping over them and circles of black beneath; lips drawn together, cruelly set; cheeks colourless; between the brows a slight furrow; and over all the waving dark hair gathered back from the low forehead.

As nearly as a man may read the soul of a woman, he had read hers, with a vision supernaturally sharpened by pain. He had seen in her face the shame, the agony of violated reserve, the bitter wounding of her pride—the pride, which for no single moment had foreseen that ending. He had known that she was thinking, "I am a thing apart, but for the accident of concealment, a thing of shame." He had recognised that in the reaction of her feelings there was a physical repulsion to himself, a desire to hurt because she had been hurt. He had understood what it was costing her to go about as usual, and keep her vizor down to the world. He had known in her a courage he did not possess himself, an untameable pride. All this he had seen in that face. That which he had not seen was the mysterious weakness of woman, the greater and the most pitiful of all qualities.

He rose from his seat, went into his dressing-room, and poured some brandy from a shooting flask. When he had drunk it he came back again to his bedroom. He walked up and down once or twice softly, clenching his hands, and mechanically taking care that his footsteps made no noise on the bare, slippery floor. Then he put his hand into the breastpocket of his coat, took out a revolver, and dropped it into the table-drawer. As he did so he gave a queer little laugh. He had carried it about with him for three days, and it was like parting with an old friend. It had been comforting to feel the weight of it in his pocket, with the thought that there was always that escape from the grinding torture of the slowly moving hours.

He shut the drawer with a bang of finality. The brandy had cleared his brain, and he saw that for several reasons the end was not that way. He must see it out. He began to perceive also that it was a grimmer and a harder thing than he had imagined for a human being to abandon hope; and yet, as the bang of the shut drawer echoed in the silent room, he felt that it was even more grim and hard to go on living. He knew all the time that, of those two thoughts, he would never find out which was the truer, because of a deeply-rooted instinct, cowardly-heroic, which would drive him to live while he was sane.

He threw himself at full length upon the floor, pressing his face into the soft rug and Shikari woke up to lick his outstretched hands. The moonlight passed on over the house and left him there.

Some time in the dense darkness he crawled to his knees, and bowed himself against the bed in a prayer, unconvinced, faithless, and voiceless, a mere straining after rest in the hard pressure of

81

his face against the cool covering of the bed, after peace in the touch of his knees upon the floor.

He fell asleep so. When he woke it was with a vague contempt of himself that had no sting in it, and, half-dressed as he was, he fell asleep again upon the bed in sheer exhaustion.

Chapter Twelve

THE sun staring into his room awoke him. As he stretched himself, the sight of his own half-dressed figure brought him with a cruel jerk to a sense of reality.

Yet, in spite of the agony of returning consciousness, there was a glow of resolution in his mind, another dawning of hope. He shrank before the acknowledgment of it. To his indolent, pleasure-loving nature, a resigned acceptance of the worst meant relief. He resented the renewed vitality which brought suspense, and a fresh struggle against the abandonment of hope. With every movement of his muscles in the morning air came another balancing of the possibilities. Effort of any sort, other than the purely physical, was painful to him; he shrank from beginning again a mental contest against overpowering odds, and all the time the struggle was renewing itself within him. It was his nature to shrink from obstacles, and to hate the rough of life, yet when he encountered it, something in him always forced him forward against his will. He began to calculate the earliest minute at which he might see Jocelyn.

He dressed hastily, swallowed some coffee and a roll, and ordered his pony. While waiting for it he paced restlessly up and down the little garden. Once, when he passed her window, he saw his wife's figure moving feebly from her bedroom to her sitting-room. He had heard her talking, had heard her cough, had even heard her laughing, but it was all he had *seen* of her for three days. He turned away hastily, and walked down into the road to wait. . . .

Four hours later the bay pony, very tired, stopped with a jerk before the villa door. The afternoon sun struck hotly on to the white road, and the palm trees by the Saracen tower were waiting dejectedly for the wind, that hung in the black clouds over the sea, to free them from their dusty covering. Giles got off, he staggered slightly, and wiped his forehead as he gave the reins to the slim, dark Italian boy who appeared like a mournful shadow from an unexpected corner to take them—then throwing his head back he walked into the house.

Shortly, this was what had happened to him in the four hours.

He had ridden at a pace alternately very fast and very slow to the Hôtel Milano. At the gate of the hotel garden the German proprietor was standing, a large, grave man, with a military back. The ladies, he said, had gone to Monte Carlo, would Monsieur not come in and rest himself from the heat, and wait, for the ladies would surely be back very presently. Monsieur would not! The ladies would certainly return for the luncheon at half-one. Yes! there was a train from Monte Carlo at twelve o'clock; it was now eleven. Would not Monsieur, perhaps, drink something—there was some very good hock newly arrived. Monsieur would not! It was very hot! *Aufwiedersehn!*

As Giles dug his heels into the pony's sides and clattered up the street towards the Cornice Road, the German proprietor, bowing his long, bearded face towards his gaunt chest, looked gravely after him.

"Mein Herr Legard is no longer the same man, I think," he said slowly to his little French wife, in an interval of her flower gathering. "He used to be so calm, so nonchalant; now he does everything *augenblicklich*, with his mouth shut and his brows down. He is ill, I think, or he has lost money."

"*Que t'es bête, mon cher!*" said Madame compassionately, a rose in her mouth, and her small, fat, French hands full of carnations.

Legard rode into Monte Carlo, he could not wait for the chance of their returning for lunch. He came upon them walking down from Smith's bank to the station. He had the privilege of shaking hands with them. Mrs. Travis was slightly in front—she had always a conviction that trains wished to elude her. After a glance at his face, she discreetly increased her pace and disappeared into the station, perceiving from its expression that she would be more comfortable away from him.

Giles was alone with Jocelyn for two seconds. He had her hand in his, a perfectly cold, motionless hand. He looked at her eyes, they were half closed and averted; a furrow was between her brows, and her lips were pressed together. He could hardly prevent himself from crying out. Jocelyn turned her eyes to his face for one second, the face of a man in purgatory, with the corners of the mouth drawn back from the clenched teeth, the chin square, the jaw quivering, the eyes deep-sunk and staring. The expression of her own face did not change, it was at once shrinking and repellent. He dropped her hand with a gasp, and sat motionless on the pony, looking after her as she walked into the station. He sat there until he saw the train go out, but she did not come back.

Then he rode slowly home along the dusty road, at the pony's own pace, bending over its neck, and staring in front of him like a man in a dream....

When he had thrown the reins to his servant he went up the steps to the house. At the top of the winding, rose-hung passage, he turned. A vision of Jocelyn, standing at the foot and looking up at him with the roses whispering above her, was for an instant before him; then it was gone, and there stood only an Italian boy, in nankeen clothes, and a wide-brimmed hat, holding the ends of the pony's reins, and looking up at his master with mournful black eyes. Legard spoke in his gentle voice. It was characteristic of him that in his trouble his consideration for others did not lessen.

"Jacopo, we shall take the yacht and go shooting."

Jacopo's apathetic, olive-coloured face lighted up for a moment. He was a silent, ubiquitous boy, and devoted to his master.

"Si, Signore!"

"We start directly—you must be ready tonight."

The boy stroked the pony's nose solemnly with his dark fingers. Giles had chosen him because he was fond of animals—a rare thing in an Italian.

"For where, Signore?" he said.

"I don't know yet; somewhere where there is something to shoot. Pack for cold weather and for hot. We shall be away a long time perhaps. Take Shikari, and put in a rug for him. That's all, I think. Do you want any money?"

"No, Signore."

Jacopo threw the reins on the pony's neck and departed,

whistling a little tune. The pony followed him like a dog.

Legard stayed a moment at the top of the steps, passing his hand over his brow, and trying to conjure up again the girl's image, then he went into the house and began mechanically to overhaul his guns.

For a little while he felt the relief it would be to have done with it all—a merciful span of time that was gone as soon as it was come—then a great horror of loneliness, and a sense that the sands of his life had run out, came over him. He leant his face against the frame of the gun cabinet, feeling sick and cold. He *could* not live without her!

A great wave of pity for her carried him a little beyond that thought. Her eyes with the shrinking look in them were always before him. At whatever cost he would not crown the disgrace of his manhood by forcing himself upon her! The instinctive revolt within him against brutality of any sort, which was at once the strength and the weakness of his character, forbade that. To that instinct he must be true! He clung to it with the despairing clutch of a man who had lost other things which he had thought secure. He would go away! He would see her once again, that very day, as a matter of form—he did not confess to any hope— just as a matter of form. He was, in fact, unable, even then, to despair. He went to the sideboard, drank some wine, and ate some fruit—he could not get anything solid down—and went about his preparations mechanically. The thought came into his mind that, since he was going away, he must see his wife. He poured out the rest of the wine, drank it, and lit a cigarette. If it had to be done, it might as well be done at once. He sat down, and smoked the cigarette steadily through, with a sense of effacing his emotions. When he had finished it he got up and knocked at her door.

There was no answer. He opened it gently and went in.

Chapter Thirteen

In the room there was a faint, sweet, sickly smell of flowers and of drugs, the scent that pervades the rooms of invalids. The sun was still blazing outside, and through the drawn Venetian blinds three long streaks of warm light forced their way, and fell across the white figure lying on the couch. Bars of golden air, breathing with innumerable tiny sparks of dust—they seemed in the hushed room to be the only living things. Even the flowers drooped, like beings that had given up their souls to the woman with the ashen yellow face, whose breathing scarcely stirred the white swansdown ruffle thrown across her chest. Over the bullfinch's cage was drawn a grey silk covering that quivered faintly at the opening of the door. The oaken furniture seemed to shrink dark and ill-defined into the corners of the room.

It was so still there that Giles paused, and his heart gave a queer thump. He shut the door noiselessly, and bent his head, looking into his wife's face. His tall, thin figure had great dignity in the dim light.

She was not dead, as he had thought, she was asleep. On the little table by the couch were the book she had been reading—Tolstoi's "The Kingdom of God is within You"—three roses, a medicine glass, and bottle. Giles's eyes fastened on the roses; by some twist of fate they were Jocelyn's favourites, the sunset-coloured Riviera roses. A bar of light fell across two of them, so that they gleamed and glowed at him; the third was in shadow, the colour drained from its petals by the blight of the grey room.

It seemed to him as an omen, and he shivered. He took the rose, and turned its face to the sunlight. His wife sighed huskily in her sleep.

Giles stepped back, he thought she would wake, but she did not. He listened to her breathing, it was faint and strained; and but for the faint, irregular monotony of it she might have been dead. She was very far from death, as it seemed to him, with the insistent pain of Jocelyn's suffering, and the lurking shadow of possible shame ever present to his mind.

A faint sound of voices rose in the outer corridor, and footsteps creaked coming down the passage towards the door. Giles stepped behind a screen, which sheltered the couch from a French window opening on the garden. His nerves were so jarred and unstrung that he recoiled from the idea of meeting any one, and having to talk in his wife's presence. The clasp of the window was not fastened; it was slightly ajar. He waited, prepared to step out if any one came.

The door was opened softly, and he heard a whispered conversation in French.

"Madame is asleep, Monsieur."

"Ah! then do not wake her for the world! I will call again later. It is of no consequence. I will take a little walk. Thank you, Pauline; shut the door gently."

Giles recognised the peculiarly soft, purring tones of Nielsen's voice. The door closed softly, and through the flower-covered trellis work, he watched the Swede's square figure as he tiptoed his way down the steps. He noticed black clouds creeping fast towards the coast from over the sea, and the olives below the road beginning to sway a little. He saw very clearly, and with a childish feeling of irritation, Nielsen's broad, wrinkled face, with its great tawny moustache and gold-rimmed eyeglass, lifted towards the sky at an angle which bared his short neck.

His brain was in an exhausted state of nervous excitement, rendering it as receptive of outward impression as a photographer's plate; everything he saw and heard was graven upon it indelibly.

When Neilsen had disappeared, Giles turned back to his wife's couch. The bars of sunlight were gone. She was still sleeping heavily; would she never wake, and let him get this over?

He fingered the medicine glass mechanically, there were a few drops of moisture at the bottom. He smelled it—the sickly-sweet, unmistakable smell of morphia—and put it down with a faint quiver of disgust. The drug she took every day to make her sleep. He looked at the bottle nearly full of a white liquid, with a kind of fascination. A tenth of it would kill him! An easy death, that! He felt with indignation that the bottle had no business to be there; his wife always put it under her cushions before going to sleep, for fear of a mistake—he had seen her many times. Fingering the cool, slippery round of the glass, he looked mechanically about him for the medicine that she took the instant she woke, heavy and dazed from the morphia. It should be there ready, it was always there! There was no bottle upon the table except the wrong one, that which should have been under her cushions.

A thought flashed though his mind, a vivid vision snatched from the future. What if—! He stood up, hardly breathing, his hands behind his back, looking down upon his wife. Her first waking act! Half conscious—the wrong bottle!—the wrong . . .

He drew a deep breath, turned suddenly upon his heel, and passed swiftly through the window.

The humming of insects and the long droning sigh of the coming wind was in the breath of the warm air as he stepped out. A creeper went swish-swish over his head, and a loosened spray of jessamine beat him in the face. Its sweet, subtle scent penetrated his senses and gave him a queer feeling as if his heart were contracting within him, and the cool beat of the leaves against his face felt like the touch of fingers, forcing him back. He pulled the window to, very gently. A chance had been sent!

A chance had been sent! He had a dim vision of black clouds driving over the sky, olives swaying in a long line in front of him, and there was the road, long, white, and dusty, and he knew that what he had to do was to get down it, as far and as fast as he could. To get down it, before he began to think. He began to run —he had no hat on, and he knew it, but he knew that it was not his business to inquire into the reason why he had no hat, it was to get over the ground quickly.

He found that he *was* thinking as he went, but upon quite trivial matters. He thought of a little shop at the bottom of the road, where he could buy himself a hat, a peasant's hat like Jacopo's; he hoped it might be clean. He thought of the weather; it looked like breaking up, the clouds made a curious effect over the sea. He thought at a great pace, as fast as he could, and his thoughts left no mark whatever on his mind.

His tall figure striding along, bareheaded, with coat flying open, created no small astonishment in Nielsen's mind, who, seated on the edge of the water-tank under the olives opposite, was waiting with his usual surface apathy to renew his visit at the villa. Remembering the scene of the night before, he made no attempt to attract Legard's attention, but sat fingering his long moustache, and staring patiently after him, with mixed feelings of curiosity and commiseration.

Giles passed the shop without stopping—he was so busy keeping his mind unoccupied—and he had to turn back to buy himself a hat. He had exhausted his power of trivial reflection now, and he tried to think of Jocelyn. He would see her— he must see her! And as he walked he found that her image, to which he trusted to save himself from thought, danced elusively just out of the reach of his mind's eye.

He walked swiftly, a man haunted by the hidden, ugly shape of an unborn remorse. At a turn in the road he came suddenly upon Jocelyn herself.

Chapter Fourteen

SHE was sitting on a stony bank covered with wild thyme, just above the road; her soft mauve blouse and the little stone-coloured toque on her head were in exact tone with their setting. Over her knees hung a long, bright spray of gladiolus flowers.

In the suddenness of the meeting, the grave dejected look on her bent face smote Giles with the vehemence of a blow. Now that what he had set himself to attain was unexpectedly within his reach, he felt as if he could not face her.

He stopped. Had she seen him? Should he go back? He half turned in his painful indecision, shuffling his feet on the dusty road.

Jocelyn raised her head. He could see her face, the eyes stared at him, unnaturally soft and large, and there was a pitiful curve at the corners of her mouth.

He felt no more indecision or dread, he felt nothing but the helplessness and pathos of her face. He brushed his hand over his eyes, walked across the road, and stood close to her, with his head bent down and his face hidden under the wide-brimmed peasant's hat.

Without saying a word she put out her hand, and her slender fingers fell like bars of ice across his burning palm. Then she said—

"Will you come with me up the hill a little? If there is peace anywhere, it will be among the olives."

His heart beat violently, giving him a sense of suffocation.

They left the dusty road, and mounted the banks silently, twisting in and out up the narrow path over slopes covered with yellow broom and magenta gladiolus, with snowy garlic flower, purple vetch, and masses of mauve wild thyme. The scent from the pine needles and the sage-plant rose from the cooling earth as the heat of the vivid, glaring day gave way under the clouds driven up by the rising wind.

At first, as they climbed the steep ascent, a rush of relief, a joyous flowing of his blood at being near her again, carried him away past all power of reason and doubt. It was happiness, just to see her slender figure swaying, as she mounted two paces in front of him, to hear her lightly-drawn breath, to catch the perfume of her hair, the half glimpse of her profile as the path twisted. But long before they stopped there had come a returning agony of doubt. What would she say when she at last spoke? What were they to be to each other in the future? Had he sinned beyond forgiveness? With one step he felt a mad spasm of hope, with the next the dull throb of a blank despair; and always with him, like the cloud left by a bad dream, was the grim shadow of his wife's awakening beside the little table, in that darkened room.

They were high up now among the olives, and neither had spoken. A gloomy, purple hue had spread like a pall over the broken ridges of the mountains, which ran inland to the west. It shaded up from the surf-girt, murky sea, and deepened on the sides of the hills till it crowned the summit with a hard, blue line against the veiled sky. Upon the remote greyness of the westward sea the hidden sun threw up a narrow streak of yellow light. Where the sun had travelled, far as the gloomy horizon, the violet waters brooded in long, broken ridges, and inshore little white waves hissed at the borders of shallow, turquoise pools.

The wind was sighing a mournful tune in gentle crescendo through the patient olives, whose knotted stems creaked a sad accompaniment. In the sinister colouring the vivid green of a tiny fig-tree made a single bright spot whereon the eye rested gratefully.

At the foot of a little tower, grey, ruined, and flanked by two towering cypresses, Jocelyn stopped, and, leaning against the broken stair, looked long and steadily over the sea. One small singing-bird was lifting the feeble requiem of the day's departed glory, and from the valley came an occasional crowing of cocks; these, and the sigh of the wind, were the only sounds. Presently she spoke—

"I like that angry white blaze on the sea," she said. Giles

heard the even tones of her voice with wonder, but they served to steady him.

"Yes, it's beautiful." He was standing beside her, a tall figure, holding his hat in his hand, and taking deep breaths like a man that has come to the surface of water, after a long dive. He found it difficult to believe that he was actually at her side talking commonplaces, and he made a great effort to brace himself to meet what was coming. His impulse was to fling himself at her feet, but he stood straight and stiff, gnawing his moustache, and clenching his hands. Presently Jocelyn said, without looking at him—

"We have something to say to each other, haven't we?"

"Yes. What made you come?"

"Your face at the station."

"Ah!"

To both of them the interchange of question and answer seemed very strange and unreal. There was another silence. Of the two faces, side by side, staring visionless over the sea, the man's showed the ravages of emotion most; perhaps because he was older, perhaps because it was his nature to take things harder. The little bird still lifted its voice; there was a curious pathos in the feeble twittering.

Jocelyn said suddenly, lifting her eyes to his—

"I have suffered so. I have cried till I think I shall never cry again. Forgive me, I didn't mean to hurt you, I didn't want to hurt you so. I couldn't help it. Poor eyes!"

Her hand stole up, and touched his face. With the words and the touch of her hands, his self-control suddenly left him, and he shook with dry, silent sobs, burying his face deep in his hands. It was characteristic of him that he broke down most at the touch of tenderness.

Jocelyn pulled his head down on to her shoulder, stroking his hair and his cheek with her fingers, and murmuring—

"There, there!" as a mother cries to her child. All the hardness had gone out of her face, it was very tender, and her eyes were pure and deep-coloured with a wonderful pity.

Making a great effort, Giles mastered himself; he put his arms round her, and stood rocking himself to and fro gently, his face buried in her hair. There was no passion in his embrace, only pity, and gradually peace.

It was a long time before either spoke again.

"My darling, forgive me!" he said at last in a faint, husky whisper, barely heard in the moaning of the wind.

"Dear, there is nothing to forgive—it was my fault—I tempted you."

Giles shuddered.

"No, no!" he said, and he pressed her convulsively in his arms.

The words came presently from him with an effort—

"Tell me, darling! Is it all pity you have for me now? Is there any love left?—tell me the truth," but he could not look at her, he dreaded the answer too much.

Jocelyn drew herself gently away from him, till only the touch of his fingers rested on her arms.

"I don't know," she said; "it isn't as it used to be—I can't tell."

He sighed.

"It isn't as it used to be—how can it be? I think something has died in me. But, dear— I know that if I did not love you, I couldn't pity you. I couldn't be sorry for you. I'm sure of that—I could only hate you."

"Thank God!" he said, breathing deeply. It was like the lifting of a great weight from his chest; but as he straightened himself, the spectre of his wife's awakening in the darkened room suddenly started up before him.

"Promise me," he said with an eager ring in his voice, "*whatever comes,* you won't shut me quite away from you! Promise you'll let me share your suffering! *Promise me*—"

She shuddered, and her eyes contracted.

"I promise," she whispered.

"Thank you, Sweet, that is sacred," he said.

He drew her again towards him, and would have kissed her lips; but she bent her forehead to him instead, and he kissed it reverently.

The wind was rising steadily, it swept through the trees, and whistled mournfully in the hollows of the ruined tower.

Jocelyn was shivering in her light blouse.

"Let me go home, there is a storm coming, and I am so tired." She spoke like frightened child.

He answered mechanically like a man in deep thought.

"Poor little one, yes, yes, at once." He was holding his watch in his hand, and looking over her shoulder down the hill side, measuring time against distance. He was thinking there would still

94

be a chance—his wife might have gone on sleeping. If he could only get back to the room in time? and he muttered to himself, absorbed in his sudden desire to get back before it was too late.

"Yes," he said, "we must go down before the storm breaks. Come, darling," and he led the way down the winding path rapidly.

When they reached the road, he said—

"Can you go home alone? You will be quite safe on the road, and I have something to do—very important, terribly important. I must go. Let me see you to-morrow. I will come, may I? Good-bye! good-bye! Poor child, you look so tired." He put his hands gently on either side of her face, looking into her eyes.

"Remember your promise!" he said, and kissed her lips passionately; then, as if some invisible force had plucked him from her, he turned suddenly and walked along the road at full speed, his head bent down, and without once looking back.

Jocelyn gazed after him surprised and trembling. The tide of her emotions had run out and left her spent and heavy with a sense of coming disaster.

Chapter Fifteen

ONCE hidden by a group of trees, Giles broke into a run. The road stared in front of him, white and implacable; the dust rose from it, choking him. He bent forward, lifting his feet doggedly, dead tired, and with the feeling that he would never get to the villa. There was a lull in the wind, and a few splashes of warm rain fell upon him.

Suddenly he stopped. What was he running for? To find out if his wife had killed herself? A mere matter of curiosity. For it came into his mind that nothing whatever was changed. He had left her to die. He was going back—to save her? A cold sweat broke out on his forehead, he leant against a pine tree by the road side and rocked himself to and fro, trying to think.

A drove of kine passed close, their bells tinkling, as one by one turned wet muzzle, and moody, brown eyes towards him. The sound, full of memory, of those bells was a spur to his thoughts. Nothing was changed! A chance had been sent to him and to Jocelyn—above all, to Jocelyn! And he was going back to set it at naught?

He had a vision of the face that he loved, as it might become, haggard and shame-ridden, and of the faces of all the people he had ever known drawn in a sanctimonious circle around it. He felt as if he were being guilty of treachery. Why should he go back? He would stifle memory—forget he had ever been in the room. It was a cowardly thought, and he knew it. He could not get away from responsibility one way or the other—he had to accept it. He seemed continually to see his wife's frail body half-raised on one bent elbow, her thin hand stretched gropingly, the long fingers closing on the medicine bottle—her face, the look of exhaustion upon it, and the heavy, half-closed eyes. He began to walk forward again, slowly at first, then faster and faster.

His mind swayed, like the olive trees in the gusty wind, this way and that. When at moments, in the black irresolution of his thoughts, he had glimpses of the knowledge that it was all decided —that he *was* going back to save her if he could—he hated himself.

The sound of a horse's gallop was in the wind that beat in his face. An undefined feeling of guilt made him stoop to avoid notice as he walked. The horseman passed; there was a cry in his ears, the single word "Madame!" He looked up sharply; through a cloud of dust he had a glimpse of flying hoofs, and of Jacopo's body turned in the saddle, waving a hand towards the villa.

Something had happened! What? Was he to go down to the grave with the memory of his desertion staring him in the face? Anything was better than this suspense. He dashed forward and arrived, breathless, and dripping with perspiration. He ran up the steps. At the window, out of which he had come, he stopped; it was as he had left it. He set his face against the glass, and stared through. He could see things in the room dimly in the grey light, her couch and figures standing beside it, the white drapery upon it, but he could not see her face.

The same spray of jessamine trailed across his cheek, a cock-chafer buzzed against him. Was it really two hours since he had left that room?

The shrill sound of a woman's sob came to him from within; it jarred his nerves, so that he started and his hand knocked against the glass. A figure inside looked up sharply with a gesture of surprise. It was Nielsen. Giles stared back at him through the window, his face, very white and motionless, still pressed against it. After a moment, when nothing in the heavens and the earth seemed to move, he pushed it open, and went in, walking unsteadily, his hands clenched convulsively on the hat in them.

"What is it?"

"Dead!"

"Ah!" There was no movement in the room save the heaving of the maid's shoulders, as she crouched by the body of her mistress.

The two men faced each other staring, the minds of both busy with a thousand thoughts, their eyes expressing nothing.

A long-drawn, quavering sob, with a gasp at the end, vibrated painfully through the silence. Giles with an uncontrollable movement put his hands up to his ears. Nielsen did not stir, but he frowned.

"You had better go, Pauline," he said to the maid, "you can be of no use till the doctor comes, then I will call you, but you must be good and quiet, you know." She rose, and went out, choking back her sobs.

Once more there was silence, and at the foot of the couch the men stared at each other. Nielsen, the shorter by four or five inches, stood gnawing his moustache, his head stiffly bent back, his hands in front of him mechanically polishing his eyeglass; his shortsighted eyes were narrowed and puckered with the effort of vision. Legard stared downwards at him, his eyes deep sunk, his hands folding and refolding his hat; his teeth were clenched, and beads of perspiration stood on his forehead.

"I don't believe—how do you know?" he said suddenly, but without looking at the couch.

"It is so, I have seen it too often. But look for yourself, I found her like that." Nielsen pointed towards the body.

"No! No!" said Giles in a harsh whisper, "that's enough." He covered his eyes with his hand, and, turning away, began to walk up and down the room. He did not once glance at the body. Nielsen watched him unobserved with a growing feeling of perplexity and of repulsion. "Poor lady!" he said softly, and sat down by the side of the couch. Bending forward with his chin in his hand, he continued to watch Giles restlessly pacing up and down the room. He was trying to put the pieces of a puzzle together in his mind. It seemed to him singular that Legard had not asked any questions; he appeared to know already. His mind reverted to the picture of him hurrying away from the villa hatless and with great strides two hours ago, and a thought struck him.

"Was your wife alive when you left her, you know—two hours ago?" he asked suddenly.

Legard stopped short in his pacing; it was as if a sudden accusation had been hurled at him.

"Yes," he said hoarsely. "That is—" He broke off. How did Nielsen know he had been with her? He clenched his jaws and the snap of his teeth together was the only sound in the silent room. For an instant he felt like a hunted man, and he glared at the Swede, waiting for the next question. But it did not come. Nielsen sat there, quietly nursing his chin and looking at the floor—the answer had told him what he wanted to know. Legard *had* been in the room, but the servants had not known it; he had come out like a man flying from the plague, and it was not an hour since he had himself found Mrs. Legard dead. She had apparently died from an overdose of morphia, for as she lay with her hand by her side, the fingers of it were still closed upon the medicine glass.

It was a singular affair; with the discretion of experience he filed it for reference, and sat quietly nursing his chin and looking at the floor.

Outside, the wind moaned and raged, and a driving rain began to beat against the windows. Inside was the stillness of death itself.

Giles had fallen into a chair with his elbows resting on the table, and his face buried in his hands. The hunted feeling of the moment had gone in a great indifference—a numb sensation that was creeping over him. What did it matter? Let the fellow think what he would, he could *know* nothing. There was nothing to know, of course—it was a matter between him and his own conscience.

He was surprised that he no longer felt pain, remorse, or indecision, only a dull craving for rest, and that peculiar numbness in his brain and limbs.

There was a sound of wheels outside—then footsteps—he heard them indistinctly through the hissing of the rain and the moaning of the wind. The door opened, and some one came into the room.

In the dim light he had an impression of a man with a bearded face and dark clothes, of water dripping from the sleeves of his coat and from his hat. A doctor! Not his wife's doctor! He was conscious, too, of the maid's presence, of low-voiced questions and answers in French, of fingers pointed at himself, of a long hush, of the lifting of something white on the couch and of its being laid gently back again.

He had an impression of being spoken to, and of answering, of the subdued rattle of Venetian blinds drawn up, of the soft beating of the rain against the window panes.

The group of figures round the couch seemed to shift and shift again. There was another long hush, then a whisper in French.

"Poor fellow, he seems quite overcome!" And another voice,

low also, and of uncertain intonation, said, *"Que voulez-vous? it is his wife."*

In a silence, that seemed everlasting, he sat staring at a black figure leaning over the couch and going through evolutions with a bottle, measuring, smelling, tasting it, bending forward till his body was right-angled, raising himself again. Then the silence came to an end in words pronounced, distinctly and with finality, in the French tongue.

"Morphia—the bottle in her hand—she was in the habit of taking it? Ah! Yes—failure of the action of the heart, no doubt an overdose—dead about an hour—poor woman—not an uncommon case."

He experienced a sensation of gratitude—the first sensation of any sort for many minutes— the affair was not eternal, he would sometime or another get rid of these people, and be left to himself and have rest. He got up slowly and with effort. Again the slurred rattle of the Venetian blinds, the rustle of a sheet drawn over the couch. Then a moment when three figures stood stiff, awkward, dismally devoid of action; a confused shaking of hands, a subdued unintelligible murmur, a glimpse of retreating figures, the fluttering whish of a skirt, the click of a closing door, and—he was alone.

Chapter Sixteen

In the early hours of the sleepy afternoon, when the June sun blazes, and the air outside is heavy with heat, the coolest place in Monte Carlo is the Casino.

At one of the few roulette tables where play was going on Nielsen sat, leaning back in his chair, his eyes half closed, and one of his hands resting upon the table.

It was only three o'clock, but he had finished work for the day. He sat on, apparently watching the game, in reality occupied in putting together the pieces of his puzzle. The polished floors, and even the garish colouring of the walls and ceilings, looked soft in the mellow light that filtered through the wire blinds set in the windows. The glass panes had disappeared for the summer, and the cooled air was sweet with the smell of flowers and shrubs. The murmuring of the few players, the monotonous scrape of the croupiers' rakes, the sing-song of their voices, and the subdued rattle of coins on the green cloth, made a sleepy sum of sound.

Nielsen found nothing to disturb his reflections. The long rows of expressionless profiles, clear-cut or indefinite to this side and that, the shifting play of light and shade on the faces opposite, all meant nothing to him—no more than the scraping of his clerks' pens and the rows of their bent shoulders mean to the merchant, or the eternal coming and going of pasty-faced assistants to the master shopman.

With him, the indifferent cry of the croupier's voice, which announced the gain of his fixed, daily wage, was the ending of all concern in the tables. Sometimes he waited the whole day for it, watching the game as a cat watches a mouse, sometimes it came in half-an-hour, but it generally came. He knew the faces of nearly all the players; the faces of the born-gamblers who were ruining themselves—lined faces that were for the most part placid with a schooled placidity, and with restless eyes that seemed to look at everything and saw nothing but the eternal shifting of fortune; the faces of the "little" players, dilettante or careless, reckless or timid—faces which expressed all the emotions in turn, and which in the days when he had thought about these things had inspired him with a deep and disheartening belief in the smallness of human nature; the faces, too, such as you may see in any thoroughfare of life, of those who sit and sit and keep your place for a louis—patient, blighted faces, brightening only and that for a second, at the sight of a client or a coin; again, the faces of such men as himself, and those so rare that he could count them on the fingers of one hand—of men who came there day after day, day after day, just as a man goes to his office or to his chambers, as habituated and as utterly indifferent to the inner life of their surroundings as any other professional man, and who, on leaving the doors of the Casino, shake the dust of it from their feet and from their minds.

Of the many things to which Nielsen had at one time or another turned his hand, journalism had had the most attraction for him. There had been a charm in having a finger, benevolent or corrective, in the pies of other people, which his own pies had never afforded him. He was by nature curiously indifferent to the turn of his own affairs, curiously alive to the weal or woe of the rest of the world. He experienced a mental glow when dealing with the problems of other people.

At this moment he was engaged upon such a one, and he was conscious of bringing a fettered intellect to the task. He was prejudiced against the man upon whose actions he was seeking judgment; prejudiced by the most hopeless of all prejudices, that of sex—jealous of him, in fact. He endeavoured to be impartial and logical, but the thing intruded itself upon him, hampered his reason, coloured his conclusions. He felt that his conviction was mainly a matter of instinct with him, but he was none the less convinced. He did not conceal from himself that he knew very little, had failed to put the puzzle together; but the impression made upon his mind by Legard's conduct was vivid and painful.

He felt certain that he had been directly, or indirectly, the cause of his wife's death. The motive lay nakedly and glaringly exposed; the man was violently in love with Jocelyn, he had known that by a jealous instinct for many weeks. He did not know that Jocelyn returned that love. To his mind it was a monstrous and a painful idea that she ever should, and as he sat there, motionless, with the monotonous hum droning in his ears, his red-brown eyes glowed angrily, and the fingers of his hand began to drum the table.

His anger was personal, but he was also, and strongly, prompted by the impersonal feeling that it was duty to interpose, as when one sees somebody running, blindfold, a great and unnecessary danger.

He would see Jocelyn, in some way or another he would warn her! He had said no word of his suspicions to anyone, for in spite of his own conviction, he saw clearly that he had nothing in the nature of legal evidence; and he was too much a man of the world to put forward what he could not substantiate.

The funeral had taken place that morning; he had attended it with the doctor who had been called in.

Irma had been buried in the English cemetery at Mentone. No one had been invited, and the only other people present had been her own doctor, two Polish friends, and Legard himself. The latter had looked worn and ill, had spoken to nobody, and had gone away alone after the funeral. He seemed to Nielsen, throughout the ceremony, like a man witnessing some scene upon the stage; he had shown no emotion. There had been amongst those present a tacit understanding that the tragic and ill-fated manner of the death should be kept a secret. The doctors referred to it as failure of the heart. He understood that it was desired to avert the possible breath of scandal from her memory.

A faint stir at the table attracted his attention; a lady was sitting down opposite to him. He was conscious of a slight shock in the recognition of Mrs. Travis. She was bending her head forward, so that all he caught was a view of a black and white bonnet over an abundant fringe, and of plump, white-gloved hands arranging nervously her gambling paraphernalia. It had seemed to himself the most natural thing in the world to change his clothes and walk straight into the Casino from the funeral, but he was not somehow prepared for the appearance of a lady whom he knew to be a connection of Legard's. After all, the thing was business to him, pleasure to her—a very different affair, as he reflected.

Mrs. Travis raised her head. In return for his bow he acquired the knowledge that her sight varied with her desires. She evidently held to the conviction that not to see was not to be seen, and held to it firmly, with a slight deepening of the red in her cheeks, and a puffing of her lips.

He smiled to himself, and rose gently from his seat. *"Cette chère dame!"* he thought. He would return her lead. He knew that her departure was fixed for the following day; he determined, therefore, to go into Mentone and call upon her. In that way he would certainly see Jocelyn alone. Upon reflection, he condoned Mrs. Travis's appearance at the tables.

He took train and went into Mentone. As he walked up from the station to the hotel, picking his way carefully over the dusty road, a very correct figure in grey clothes with a flower in his buttonhole, his heart began to beat, and his breath to come a little fast. The subtle attraction which Jocelyn had for him stirred his pulses, and shook his nerve, with every step he took towards her. He had to stop at the entrance of the hotel to steady himself before he went in.

Chapter Seventeen

It was the third day since Giles had left her on the Cornice Road, and Jocelyn had not seen him since. She had been told of his wife's sudden death. It had seemed to her like a fable with no certain meaning in it; but the news had left her strangely excited, full of fear and doubt, with the feeling that she was, like a swimmer, out of her depth and struggling in dark and uncertain waters. She longed wistfully for some glimpse into the dim future. She felt a tremulous compassion for the woman whose life had been so full of pain, whose end had been so sudden; and with that compassion was mingled a sense of remorse, of bitter regret that she had done her a great and unmerited wrong. During the first days of her own humiliation there had been no room for that feeling in the lonely stress of her spirit; now, when the tide of her shame ebbed, when the unwitting cause of that shame slipped silently and swiftly away from the reach of her secret resentment, this other pain came. But, above all else, she had a restless yearning to see Giles, to rest the burden of her grief and of her fear upon his shoulders; to shake herself once more free from this nightmare of whirling shadows and dark pitfalls, and step into the sunshine of life. She felt that he could help her, and he alone.

As she moved softly about the room arranging flowers and books with supple, slender fingers—Jocelyn's fingers were always busy, moving swiftly to their various ends—she thought for the hundredth time of the wording of the note that was folded into her dress—

"Jacopo will have told you what has happened. I could not

come yesterday, nor to-day. I will be at the hotel to-morrow at half-past four. I *must* see you alone—G.L."

At half-past four! It was four now. The minutes seemed leaden-winged.

She wandered to the window, and stepped out on to the stone terrace where the sun beat fiercely. She felt its fiery touch upon her face, upon her arms and neck through the thin muslin of her dress, and her spirits rose insensibly. Those were right who worshipped the Sun! It was he who brought colour to the rose, song to the air, life to the blood! He who sailed high in the heavens to warm and cherish when the world was dark and dreary! She leaned against the window, looking up at the yellow roses trailing above her head, and humming to herself.

Nielsen, whom the servant had shown into the room unannounced, stood looking at her a long time. He was thinking that never in his life had he seen anything prettier than the line of her slender, rounded throat, and of her pointed chin thrust softly forward. Her lips were slightly parted in the act of singing, but he could not hear her. The light went out of her face as quickly as it had come; with a sigh she bent her head, and moved restlessly back into the room.

Nielsen stepped forward; he had seen the bright look upon her face in the streaming sunlight, the sudden cloud that passed over her eyes and the droop of her mouth; and when she came to him with a smile and some commonplace remark of greeting, he experienced a feeling of discomfiture, a sense of having hit up against something hard and impassable. What did he, with all his experience, know of women?—of this girl, upon whose face he had seen a moment before the stamp of life, and who veiled it from him impenetrably with a smile? What had he come to see her for? To offer her a warning? To do it delicately and diplomatically? Fool! when with the touch of her fingers upon his, cold and light though it was, his head was going round! He saw that he had come rather to tell her how he could never forget her, would follow her, until some day or other she cared for him as he cared for her! The idea that she was going away from him, out of his reach, that he would no longer be able to come and see her daily, when he wished—was suddenly and crushingly brought home to him, as he looked at her slender figure in its soft, grey dress, and at the little head poised so erect and so daintily upon it.

"Won't you sit down?"

Again, the sense of being baffled, of encountering a barrier. Yes, he would sit down, many thanks!

"And how is the dear aunt? And we shall lose you to-morrow, everything that makes life endurable?" And so on, and so on, in purring tones rolling his r's. It was such a habit of his to talk, that he went on uttering smooth commonplaces and looking unutterable things—feeling all the time that he would give the world for a moment of silence in which to steady himself, and find out exactly what he wished to say, and how to say it.

Jocelyn had seated herself at her piano with her face half turned over her shoulder towards him, and while she answered him her fingers touched the notes silently. His eyes fastened on them, the swift, silent fingers that seemed to be keeping him at bay.

It roused a sudden feeling of anger in him. He would not—was there nothing in her he could touch, in those eyes that looked at him so coldly? He stopped talking, breathing quickly—he felt quite out of breath. A low chord, suddenly struck, vibrated softly through the room. He rose half way from his seat with his hands stretched out to lay them upon her.

She began to speak. What was she saying? He sank back again.

"Mr. Nielsen, I want you to tell me about poor Mrs.—poor Irma's death. Jacopo told me you were there."

"Ah! poor lady! a dreadful thing!" He looked at her face tense and compassionate, and was doubtful of what he should tell her.

"But how did it happen? You *were* there, weren't you?" she said.

"Well, no! I was not exactly there at the time, you know. It so happened that I came to call soon after she died. I was the first to find her."

"But what was it? Why was it? It was so dreadfully sudden."

"She died about three o'clock on Tuesday afternoon, you know. It was verry terrible—verry sad—the heart?" he stammered. Looking at the white, sensitive face that hung upon his words, he had decided to lie about that tragic ending, but it was not easy to do so to her, and he stammered.

"Is that all?" The words were so incisive, the sentence so short that it gave him no time.

"It was morphia," he said with a sudden, overwhelming

conviction that lying was futile. "Poor lady! An overdose, don't you know—she was in the habit——"

"Morphia!" her voice took the word from his, and echoed it in a whisper, and her eyes, large and dark, stared at him out of a face that was suddenly very white and still.

"Yes, an overdose, you know, quite an accident—er-r—" for the life of him he could not go on, with those frightened eyes staring into his.

There was silence, and he shifted his eyeglass methodically from one eye to the other, because, being damp with perspiration, he could not see through it. He tugged at his moustache—the girl's face was so tragically still and white.

A terrible thought had been stricken into Jocelyn's mind—the thought of suicide. What if she were the cause of this death—this overdose! It was a dreadful—an inconceivable—thought! What if, knowing everything, Irma had chosen this solution of the question! A murderess! The only motion she made in the hideous turmoil of her spirit was to clasp her hands together in her lap.

The sight of those interlacing fingers was very pitiful to Nielsen. He saw that he had touched some spring of painful feeling, the depth of which he could not sound. Why, in the name of God, had he not had the grace to lie? His feelings were a strange jumble of disgust with himself, perplexed pity, irritation that he could not read her feelings, and an aching conviction that he was beyond the pale, and entered not at all into the situation.

Jocelyn sat motionless, she would have given the world to be able to get up and walk about the room, for swift motion of any sort, to free her from the longing to scream that caught her by the throat, and made her feel breathless and suffocated. Why did not this man go and leave her alone? Alone with that thought! What was he staring at her for through that idiotic glass? Did he think she was going to faint? She wished she could. Why was she so tough that she was denied that relief?

She had an inclination to laugh wildly; she gave a little gasp. There was the sound of a closing door, and the laugh died on her lips. Nielsen, following the sudden eagerness in her eyes, turned, and saw Legard coming in. He seemed taller than ever in his black clothes, and his eyes looked straight past the Swede at Jocelyn.

Nielsen shot a quick glance at the girl. She stood waiting, her face was changed—different to the face he knew; on it was a curious look that baffled his comprehension, the eyes seemed to speak of entreaty, of fear, and of a something unfathomable beyond. Ah! they were wonderful eyes, wonderful! But they had forgotten his very existence.

He turned very pale, and rose from his chair, picking up his hat. He bowed low over it and said—

"If you will excuse me—I am sure Monsieur Legard has much to say, perhaps later—I may be permitted to bid you good-bye." He moved slowly to the window, and passed through it on to the terrace.

As he turned round to close the window after him, his immovable face, pale and wrinkled in the glaring sunshine, looked in upon them with weary, half-closed eyes. Behind that mask a consuming rage of jealousy leapt up, and fought to find expression.

Chapter Eighteen

Jocelyn remained standing where she was. Half-an-hour ago she would have run to Giles and flung herself into his arms, now she stood and looked at him, her hands clasped in front of her, waiting for the cloud of that terrible thought to pass by and let a gleam of daylight through.

"Dear, what is it, are you ill?"

Neither his voice, low and tender, nor the look of love in his eyes, nor the warm clasp of his hand upon her icy-cold fingers, were of any avail.

She drew her hands away from him and passed them over her brow, as if to sweep aside her thoughts.

"Let us go out—I want air. I can't breathe in here, come!" The words were wild, but she was surprised at the even tones of her own voice. She had thought, if she once opened her lips, she must scream. She took her hat from the table and put it on, even glancing in the glass to set it straight. Her face seemed to her very much the same as usual—that was curious!'

She led the way from the room, and into the hotel garden. Legard followed, bewildered and heavy at heart. Jocelyn walked swiftly, taking a little, stony path which ran winding upwards from the garden. Walls hemmed it in, and it was rutted where the water coursed down it in the heavy rains. It led to terraces of olive and almond trees sloping up the hill. She stopped in the shade of an old tree; she felt giddy and faint, and was glad to sit down. Giles threw himself beside her, waiting for her to speak. The brown lizards chased each other among the stones. Bees, hovering over the wild thyme, drummed softly with their wings; a cicala churred harshly from a branch above, and from far away came the faint, shrill strains of a goatherd's pipe. A thin, brown haze of heat hung over the white buildings of the town below, and the sunlight threw delicate shadows from the trees on to the stone-strewn banks of rough grass.

Presently Jocelyn raised her arm and rested it against the mossy stem of the olive tree. She looked dazed, like one who had received a heavy blow, and she kept glancing from side to side, as if trying to find the way out of some unfamiliar place.

"When did Irma die?" she said suddenly.

Legard winced, he tried to answer steadily and without emotion, but there was fear in his heart, fear of her reading that which lay between him and his conscience.

"On Tuesday afternoon."

"What did she die of, it was very sudden? Mr. Nielsen told me that—that—she took an overdose of morphia." She spoke with hesitation, but hurriedly, as if afraid to give him time to deceive her. "Was it true?" she said, without looking at him.

"Yes," muttered Giles. He also looked away. The mind of each of them was fixed solely upon its own grim terror, neither saw the spectre imaged in the thoughts of the other.

"She knew—everything?" Jocelyn said. It sounded like the expression of a conviction rather than a question.

"I don't know—perhaps—I think so," and he looked at her swiftly with a catch in his breath, for the spectre of her thoughts had peeped out at him, and he was very frightened.

"Look at me, darling!" he said pleadingly.

She looked at him, and across his mind fell the shadow of what lay before him.

"Good God! what are you thinking?"

"I am thinking," said Jocelyn simply, "that I killed her—that's all."

It was not her words that frightened him so much as her face. There was a dead look upon it, a dreadful, weary look, of something more than ordinary despair, of something fundamental, the expression of that hopeless taint of inherited fatalism, which he recognised dimly, and feared, as children fear the dark. For he could not comprehend it, his whole nature revolted—it was the point at which their individualities diverged. *His* instinct was to fight for his happiness, to fight for it with pain and trouble—*hers* to fold her hands, and let it drift to her or away.

It flashed across his mind that he had seen the same face somewhere, graven in stone, dead, immutable, the face of an image. Where, he could not say, but he had seen it. The thought frightened him the more. He was like a man fighting a nightmare, knowing all the time that it was something unreal, and suffering just the same. He felt that somewhere there must be the words, the words to break the despair of her face, to bring it back to life, to wrest the shadows from below the brown eyes that stared before them, large, lustreless, and pitifully hopeless, if only he could find them. Every man knows that feeling, that desperate search for just the right words, and sometimes they do not exist. He wracked his reason.

"My darling," he cried, "it's not true. Do you hear me, it's not true—don't yield to such a feeling, it's dreadful. Fight against it, for God's sake."

He took her in his arms, she lay passively in them. He kissed her lips, her eyes, her hair—she yielded soft and unresponsive. Her face never changed.

"It was an accident. I know it, she would never have committed suicide! never! She had strong views about that—she was too religious, besides—" The fatuity of his words choked his utterance. Words! words! of what use were words against the whole bent of a nature? and he clenched his hands in despair. He would have given anything to penetrate for one moment the mystery of her being, to enter in, and share its isolation, to know the very springs of its instincts, that he might learn how to fight them.

In the stillness of the waning day he sat with his head in his hands, thinking, always thinking. The bees droned their dreamy song, and the world was flooded with a mellow, evening light.

It was no help to him that he was fighting an unreality, it only maddened him, made him desperate. In some moments if a man be tender-hearted, everything else goes by the board. He could not bear the sight of her suffering, he felt that he *must* pierce through that terrible calm, make her *feel*, it seemed to him a matter of life or death. He saw that there was one chance, suicidal and desperate, a chance that might mean the destruction of her love for him. He would have to take it, he could not sit there looking at the weary despair of that beloved face, feeling the tragedy she would carry away in her heart. He *must* tell her the truth. Half truths were no good. He must show her the whole, naked, sordid truth. The truth which he had intended should go down with him to the grave. Perhaps she would believe that.

Two lizards, meeting suddenly, began to fight furiously in the sunlight within three paces of them; he noticed them, and wondered dully which would win. Then he began to speak in a low matter of fact voice.

If he must tell her, he thought it should be in a way that would carry conviction. The sun glared into his eyes, and he pulled his hat low upon his forehead, with a feeling that he would, at all events, hide from her the foreboding of defeat that was in them.

"Are you listening to me?" he said.

She bent her head, and he went on—

"I'll tell you the truth. I never meant to tell you, but I must, because of this dreadful idea you have in your head." Something clicked in his throat, but he threw up his head and that freed his voice. "D'you remember my leaving you on the road last Tuesday? I was going back then—to see—if I had killed her."

Jocelyn shivered and made a motion as if she would have stopped him, but he went on speaking fast and evenly.

"That afternoon about three o'clock I went into her room. She was asleep—you know she took morphia every day to make her sleep. Every day, when she woke, she had to take a dose of another medicine, I've seen it dozens of times. She used to put the morphia under her cushions before going to sleep, for fear of taking it by mistake, I've seen that too. She always woke dazed, you see; she knew the danger of taking the wrong; I remember her telling me of it once." His voice sounded to himself brutally matter of fact. He stared straight in front of him, plucking up the stiff grass by handfuls. "By some accident that day she left the morphia bottle on the table by her side, and"—he cleared his throat—"the other medicine wasn't there." Even the humming of the bees seemed to him to have ceased; he must speak the words into the silence of a breathless world. The lizards still fought in the sunshine.

"I—I saw what would happen—I knew it would kill her. I did nothing, I walked out of the room—I left her to die. Then I met you—you remember?" He forced himself to look at her face. There was no sign in it that she had even heard him.

"Don't you see?" he cried, "*I* killed her—" And he thought, "Have I gone through this for nothing?"

If she would only speak—move—do something!

"Don't you believe me?"

"Yes." The yellow sunlight played upon her face through the leaves, but its expression was unchanged.

He had a sudden, sickening foretaste of the knowledge that the real suffering of man must be worked through in an isolation grim as the grave itself. He had robbed himself for ever of any claim to her respect, to her love, and—for no use. He wondered that she did not shrink from him; he would have rather she did—it would have shown him that her will was still struggling for existence. "Jocelyn," he cried, "for God's sake, say something."

'You did it for me," she said at last, "it is all the same, you see; she died because of our sin, what does it matter whether it was by her own act, or by yours, or by mine? The shadow will always be there—always—always between us, setting us apart."

It was a relief to hear her voice, even though the words were dreadful to hear. He got upon his feet, and paced to and fro, his face lined and twisted with thought, his lips quivering below the line of his dark moustache. The lizards, always fighting, darted between the stones.

"What is to be done, then?" he said, stopping in front of her, his tall, black figure between her and the sunlight.

"You must let me go, and forget me," she said.

"My God! I can't," and he threw himself at her feet, his hands clasped on her knees, his eyes fixed on hers with a wild, despairing entreaty. "Jocelyn—darling—I can't—I *can't!*" and the goat-herd's pipe sent back a faint echo to that bitter cry.

She shivered, and her eyes contracted as if with unbearable pain; then she put out her hand, and touched his hair, it calmed him at once, but he clung to her.

"If you love me," she said in a half choked voice, "be brave. I *can't* bear any more. I can't face it—I must hide. I must go away, and hide from it."

"My darling, you promised not to shut me away."

"I can't help it, I can't *share* suffering, it's not in me. I must bear it by myself—I know it."

He would have cried again in words of entreaty and reasoning, but she stopped him, rising to her feet.

"Give me an address, I will write to you. I promise to let you know what becomes of me."

"You promise to tell me truly of yourself—everything—" his voice failed him. There was a film over his eyes, and he staggered from giddiness as he got up.

"Yes—everything," she said very low, and the words seemed hardly to escape the barrier of her lips.

"Am I never to see you, never? My God! that is hard—"

"I *must* be away from everything that reminds. I must hide. I *will* forget. Can't you see that I shall go mad? I *must* have time." Her voice rose hysterically for the first time, and she twisted her hands.

"Yes, sweet! I know, I know—" He soothed her like a child, and, with the need for that soothing, he felt some strength returning to him. He knew that he must use it quickly before it left him again.

'I will send you my address to-night," he said, "I shall go away to-morrow. You promise to write. Go, dear, I won't come with you."

He caught her suddenly in his arms, and held her face to his, kissing it passionately. The tears ran down his face and wetted her cheeks—her eyes were dry.

"God keep you—remember I am always yours, to do as you please with."

She did not speak. Her mournful eyes were lifted for a moment to his, the shadow of a smile quivered pitifully on the curve of her lips, and she was gone from his arms.

He flung himself upon the ground, and buried his face in the grass.

Part III

Chapter Nineteen

IT was the last day of March in the following year. A day when spring drew its breath even in London streets. The evening was drawing in, but the daylight still crept colourless into a pretty room high up in some mansions overlooking the river. Jocelyn Ley sat in front of the fireplace, her elbows resting upon her knees and her chin sunk in her hands. Between her arms a grey kitten lay on its back, blinking its dubious eyes, and clawing the air vaguely with one paw. The spitting flames of a wood fire leaped joyfully in a deepening blaze, and there was a scent in the room, sweet and pungent, of burnt pastilles.

At a little table, where she could catch a full light from the bay window, Mrs. Travis bent over the skeleton of a garment.

"If I take it in in the neck, I must let it out under the arms, and that means taking the sleeves out," she was saying plaintively.

Jocelyn, from her chair, murmured, "Poor dear!" She always treated her aunt with complacent tenderness, as if she were some kind of elderly child. At the same time, if there were anything to be decided upon, she invariably deferred to her opinion, not from respect, but from an inherent dislike of making herself unpleasant —which her aunt by no means shared. Jocelyn was always plastically under the domination of the nearest personality.

"That comes of not being in Paris," she went on. "You *know* you can't get a jacket in London for that price, which doesn't want altering. I'll do it for you presently when the puss is asleep."

Mrs. Travis, turning the garment this way and that, and screwing up her eyes, broke into fragmentary praise of Parisian dressmakers. They were so smart—so cheap, considering—so *chic*, pronouncing it so as to leave upon the mind an impression of yellow fluff and broken egg-shell. Jocelyn stroked the kitten's furry chest softly.

"Why aren't we in Paris?" she sighed. "I can't think what made you take this flat for so long! Chelsea's nice *for* London, but I'm so sick of London!"

Mrs. Travis sat back in her chair with a faint rustling of silk and a creaking of stays. She said "Oh!" in a funny little voice, fidgeted her hands once or twice on the table, and then folded them over the garment upon her lap. She was not really thick-skinned. If people differed or found fault with her, she suffered severely, until she had time to see that her own view was the right one. She never admitted herself in the wrong. There was no credit due to her for that, she had simply never learned how. Things might seem against her—in fact, they frequently did—but she was always inwardly convinced that she was in the right. If it had appeared to her that the world was flat, she would have admitted the imparted knowledge that it was round, with a complacent "Yes—it may be so," but she would have known it to be flat all the same.

She had a queer method of argument too. She would admit everything with a tentative "Yes," propose some remedy that wildly exceeded necessity; and when this was rejected she would fall back upon things as they were. She had a really fine turn of obstinacy, bone-obstinacy. As to the after effect upon her of argument, there was none.

A short and significant silence followed, while her skin hardened.

"You know I haven't got any money," she began at last in a smoothly injured voice. "I can't bear owing anything. I wasn't brought up to it, *and I can't do it.*" Her green eyes seemed to deprecate the possibility of disbelief, but there was nothing except the back of Jocelyn's head to deprecate, as she leant forward in her chair, and gazed at the fire with moody eyes.

The flames licked the logs, and an occasional red spark darted forth, trying to reach her outstretched feet. The kitten purred softly. Jocelyn's silence was discomfiting to Mrs. Travis; her eloquence felt faint for lack of contradiction. She began to fan herself slowly with a newspaper and to get a little red.

"You should think more of other people," she began again.

"You know I can't afford to go abroad. That horrid place has ruined me. I've never had any money, to spare, since." When Mrs. Travis lost all her money, her Puritan education enabled her to see that gambling was immoral—until she had some more. Just now she had some more, but not quite enough—a tight place for her principles.

"It's not like it used to be there. They try to get everything they can out of one. *I don't think it's right.*" These words with her conveyed the acme of disapproval. She began to enlarge upon the possibility of corrupt croupiers, weighted tables, pre-arranged cards —devices with refutation writ large upon their faces—but very dear to her. She pouted her lips as she spoke, her hands moved restlessly, and her green eyes kept glancing from the back of Jocelyn's head to her own lap—sure signs that she was agitated. She ended by declaring with decision that she would never go near the place again.

"I am glad of that," said Jocelyn quietly. She frowned, as she gazed at the dull glow playing fitfully on the charring logs. There was a minute or two of silence. A hundred memories were thronging in the girl's mind, ghosts of long hours when the sun had blazed, mocking the torment of her spirit, when the star-flecked vault of the heavens had looked down, cold and pitiless, upon her shame and misery. She put her hands over her face.

Presently there came a sudden, uneasy creak from the chair where Mrs. Travis was sitting—one would not have ventured to predict its meaning—and she began to speak.

"You've not been looking very well lately, my dear," she said with a little tentative cough. "I think perhaps we ought to go south for Easter. 'Monte' is nice, then, just for a week."

Jocelyn did not speak for a minute. She could not control her voice, and it trembled when she answered—

"You can go, of course, if you want to, I shall stay here. I *hate* the place." She got up. "I thought you said just now you were never going there again!" As she spoke, she walked across to the window. Throwing it open, she stood leaning against it, looking out over the river.

Mrs. Travis sniffed subduedly with surprise and anger. It was unlike her niece to oppose her, it was unlike her to speak with emotion. She collected herself in her chair. On this occasion, it must be confessed, it took her while a person might count ten to see that she had not contradicted herself. Then she rose from her seat, the uncompleted garment in her hand. Throwing her feet out well in front of her, she walked to the door, an imposing figure in black silk.

"It was entirely on your account," she said with dignity, opening the door, and going out with a rustle of offended petticoats.

Jocelyn, left alone, shrugged her shoulders. The grey kitten had followed her across the room, and was rubbing its arched back against her dress. She stooped, and picked it up.

She felt very lonely. The soft west wind driving the broken sky over the grey, untroubled river, was sweet with the mysterious scent of growing things, of the sap in the trees, of the earth after rain, of the flow of life; the spring scent that seems to tell us to begin again, stirs the blood to vague, unimaged longing, grips our hearts with a sweet aching.

It was the meeting of the lights—the buildings and chimneys loomed from across the river like shadowy monsters, peering into the dusk with reddening eyes. The lighted lamps on the steadfast bridges seemed to her to fling their greetings from one to the other, daring in linked chains the gathering gloom. She counted three barges, huge, amphibious beasts, creeping, black and sluggish, up river against the ebbtide. The dull hoot of a distant steamer, plying westwards, was carried now and again to her ears on the wind. The streets murmured ceaselessly from the back, roosting sparrows twittered sleepily in the trees, and from the square tower of the old church came a chime of Lenten bells. She leaned over the balcony. The bare boughs of the trees in the garden below swayed slowly. One by one the lamps of the embankment flared up; and beyond, under the drift of the restless sky, under the breath of the homeless wind, the river flowed, grey and untroubled, to the sea. The river, grey with the knowledge of the meanness and tragedy of life, untroubled in its strength and in its constancy; a philosopher to whom men confide all secrets, the recoil of the fainting spirit, the stirring of great endeavours; an image of human life, unceasing in the ebbing and flowing tides of surface emotion, whereon the traffic of living shifts to and fro, resistless in its unseen stream which is ever compelled to that mysterious sea where truth lies hidden, where life ends and life begins. Tears started into the girl's eyes. The vague solemnity of the evening, the soft breath of spring in the air, bewildered her. She had a longing to know what it all meant, to *feel* the life stirring in that width of darkened water, in the flashing, yellow lights, in the wind that fanned her flushed face. She stretched out her arms with a sudden movement, and thought, "Ah! not to be so terribly alone!" Surely, all that she saw, felt, heard, could give her some companionship!

The wind fanned and passed her by, the lamps shone with a hard light, the river flowed cold and relentless. No truth, no life, no solace! She was alone! She turned away with an aching, as if some one had struck her in the chest.

She sat down at her piano, and began to play, a rhapsody of Brahms. The chords rang full and true and under her slender fingers, the passionate throb of unending life seemed to beat in them. It was as though Nature were singing a song of full rejoicing, in the echoes of lofty mountains, in the rustling of yellow cornfields, in the medley of river torrents, and the hush of the unstained sea.

She played with her head bent a little forward, and with parted lips, and her dark eyes seemed trying to reach, beyond the music of the notes, a secret, mysterious and unfathomable. She was lost in the melody which swelled quivering into the room. When she had played the last bar, she left her hands nerveless and cold upon the keys. Suddenly, she bent her head down upon them in an uncontrollable burst of weeping. It seemed to her that all around the pulse of life was throbbing, in herself alone it stood still. . . .

A long ten months of a struggle to forget, spent in the daily society of a lady, kind-hearted, but to whom an inscrutable Providence had given as much spiritual insight as to a sack of potatoes, had told upon her strength and her nerves. She had had no support except in her own indomitable pride. Of acquaintances she had many; of friends, from the wandering manner of her life, few, and those not at hand. Religion was an empty word with her, she had never come into contact with it. She had, indeed, a love for art, but neither energy nor strength of will to study consistently.

From time to time she gave herself up to music, working from morning till night at Brahms, Schumann, Chopin, or Bach to the great discomfort of her aunt, who fidgeted in her seat at Brahms or Chopin, well-nigh howled at Bach, and would plaintively murmur requests for "The Bee's Wedding," upon which she had been brought up. She went to as many concerts as she could, and even once persuaded Mrs. Travis to accompany her. That lady sat through a magnificent performance with resigned placidity, saying from time to time "Very nice" in a drooping voice; and as they came out, gathered her black silk skirts vigorously in both hands, and stepping, large and brisk, through the crowd, remarked with relief, "There'll be just time to call at Louise's about my new bonnet!"

Jocelyn had never the heart to ask her to go again. All the same, a few days afterwards Mrs. Travis had suddenly passed a criticism upon an intricate passage of the music—a criticism which just missed being masterly. An astounding lady!

At first, it seemed long ago now, when memory was roused in her, Jocelyn had shrunk from the violent despair of her own moods; they were followed by days of headache and exhaustion, when nothing seemed to matter at all, except to feel well. Then would come days, and even weeks, when she would fling herself into the life of the passing moment, and almost forget; but always there seemed a blight over life—nothing, not even music, had any meaning; everything passed her by and left her untouched, with a sense of incompleteness. She recalled the old days, when each event and each pleasure had been, as it were, stamped with its meaning in large surface letters, and wondered.

She had kept her promise to Giles. She wrote once a month, giving him a bare chronicle of her movements and doings, at a great cost to herself; and yet, perhaps for that very reason, she would not willingly have given up writing. She would think of him sometimes with pity, often with longing, again with a wayward and inconsistent anger.

Why did he not write?

She had begged him in her first letter not to answer; and he had obeyed. The pessimism of her native distrust always besieged her.

He could not care—no man would care for so long! She wanted him, and she did not want him. For the last month she had not written; she had no longer those violent moods of despair, but she had felt too profoundly discouraged.

She had grown thinner and paler, and her face was hardly ever without its look of defeat. Her aunt's personality seemed altogether too much for her in these days; she had a feeling of suffocation and of great loneliness.

She would sit at the window sometimes for hours, watching the river, longing to get away upon it to the sea, far away to the East, to countries where no one knew her, where the sun was bright, and she might begin her life again. At other times she knew that even *that* could not give her what she wanted, or fill the vague longing within her. The winter months in London had been dreary and terrible, but her heart had never ached as now, when the spring wind stirred, and the sap coursed in the budding trees. . . .

Presently she lifted her face, flushed and tear-stained. She went to the glass and arranged her hair—she had a horror of public emotion. Her aunt would be coming back! She took up a piece of work, and began passing the needle mechanically in and out—it was almost too dark to see.

The door was opened. She expected to hear her aunt's smoothly offended voice, but the servant announced—

"Mr. Nielsen!"

Chapter Twenty

JOCELYN rose from her seat, stretching out her hands, as Nielsen came slowly forward from the door. The two peered at each other in the dusk. The servant, going out, turned up the light, and it leaped suddenly forth from the twisted brackets on the walls upon the man's square figure, and the girl's flushed and smiling face.

Nielsen bowed low over her hand with his elaborate courtesy. There was an air of prosperity about him. He was tightly buttoned into a smart, grey overcoat, and wore an orchid in his button-hole. He carried in his hand a hat of exceptional glossiness, to which a mourning band only succeeded in giving an additional air of festivity. His face was rather fatter, his moustache seemed, if anything, tawnier. His eyeglass was carefully screwed into his eye, and he regarded Jocelyn through it with an expression of admiring benevolence.

"I am verry fortunate! verry fortunate," he kept repeating, purring his r's and spitting his t's. "What a pretty room! How well you are looking!"

Her face was burning, and her eyes dark and soft after the flow of tears.

"I'm very glad to see you again," she said. "Come and sit down." She took the hat out of his hand, put it on the table, and turned a chair for him to the fire, talking all the time. In the restless and excited state of her nerves, he was a godsend to her.

"And how is the dear aunt?" he said, with his old pathetic emphasis. Jocelyn began to laugh. She could not help it—she had been waiting for the words. She struggled with her laughter and laughed the more. Nielsen looked at her rather puzzled, and then began to laugh too. He had not the least idea why, except that she looked so charming, with the bright colour in her cheeks, with her brown eyes dancing, and her white teeth showing as she swayed gracefully backwards and forwards in her chair.

"I am so sorry!" she gasped. "What *is* the matter with me? Auntie's very well, she always is, you know. Now tell me all about yourself, every little last thing."

"*Place aux dames*, my dear young lady! You will have a grreat deal of news to tell me, I am sure."

"Oh no! I've *no* news, except that I'm bored—terribly bored with London. Now come, begin! First of all—how is the 'system'?"

She leant forward, in an attitude of correct listening with a perfectly grave face.

Nielsen spread his fingers, and then gave his moustache a prolonged twist.

"Ah! *rien ne va plus!* That is all over," he said mournfully, with a little shake of his head. "I am quite lost without it. *Mais que voulez-vous?* My uncle dies—I told you of him—my uncle—did I not?—ah! the good old fellow! He leaves me a little—but yes, a little fortune. Can one go on playing a 'system'? One has one's brread and butter." He spread his fingers again. "It is inconceivable, don't you know."

"That's very good news, I'm *so* glad!"

Nielsen shrugged his shoulders gently, his head a little on one side.

"It gives me the good fortune to see you again," he said, "but for the rrest, I am not sure. It was a *verry* good 'system'; and now, you know, I have nothing to do. I am not used to that."

Jocelyn smiled, the death of the "system" amused her. "I don't think you will be idle long," she said, "you are busy by nature."

Nielsen bowed.

"And you?" he said. "Where have you been all this long time? *Mon Dieu!* Is it possible it is not yet a year?"

"We came to London first. Then in August we went to Whitby, and stayed six weeks, and got shrivelled by the winds. Then we were in Paris a month, and we've been here ever since November. How long have you been in England?"

"I arrived yesterday. I have been in Stockholm. One of my cousins had got into a—what do you call it—a hole, *une affaire de cœur*. I had a grreat deal of trouble to extrract him." He talked of his cousin as if he had been a tooth, and soon found himself giving her an account of delicate matters in which a woman figured discreditably. Jocelyn was so sympathetic a listener, and so devoid of prudery, that insensibly one told her almost anything. She inspired a sense of comradeship.

He finished, however, by saying: "I suppose I should not have told you this yarrn. It has been on my mind a grreat deal, you see, so you must forgive me."

At this moment tea arrived, followed by Mrs. Travis. She had changed her costume for a robe having a breastplate of many colours, and came in smiling affably above it. She greeted Nielsen with a smoothly dignified cordiality. She managed at the same time, by refusing to look at her niece above the waist, to convey to her a sense of unforgiven injury. For a large lady she was inimitably quick of expression—she never wasted time. She began to talk to Nielsen of old days and mutual friends; no allusion was made to the Legards, but in the middle of the conversation Jocelyn rose, and, on the pretence of drawing the blinds, went to the window. She dreaded to hear Giles's name, fearing for her self-command.

It was almost dark now. Through the dim shapes of the tree branches the black water was seen spangled with the reflections of lights, the deep rumble of a heavy cart absorbed all other sounds. The wind had dropped, and a soft grey haze was creeping downwards from the clouds.

Nielsen came over presently, and stood beside her.

"That is verry interrresting," he said. "Nothing is plain except the black water beyond. Ah! it is like the attitude of our minds looking out into life, don't you know."

Jocelyn was faintly surprised; it was a remark unlike what she knew of him, but before she could answer he was saying good-bye.

"Good night! my dear young lady. It is verry late. If you will permit me, I will say *au revoir*. I shall be at your disposal whenever you wish for an escort. I hope you will take pity upon me now that I have lost my occupation. I should like to see some pictures, and hear some music again; it is so long since I have heard any good music. Some day I trust you will come with the dear aunt and dine with me. I am staying at the Grrand, don't you know—the cōōking might be better, but then in London!"

He spread his fingers and departed.

. . . . .

During the weeks that followed they saw a good deal of Nielsen. He generally contrived to present himself, by arrangement or otherwise, in the course of the day. He appeared to divide his time between visiting them, and running all over London in search of old acquaintances whom he had known in the days when, as Bohemian and journalist, he had maintained a hand-to-mouth existence. He had lived in London for several years; he had shoals of these acquaintances, and the larger number of them, from the tales which he confided to Jocelyn, seemed to have holes in their personalities which required patching. He would get as far as the holes in his confidences, indeed he would enlarge upon them pathetically, but it was only by inference that she gathered the patches. The patching, moreover, was not confined to money transactions. He had a knack, in the service of other people, of rushing in where angels feared to tread.

Upon one occasion, when they had been lunching with him at a distinguished restaurant, they were mildly astounded by the waiter, who brought them coffee, touching their host gently upon the shoulder. Nielsen had stared at the man for a short time in a gradually dissolving indignation, risen abruptly from his seat, shaken him warmly by the hand, and retired with him into a corner of the room, where an animated conversation had ensued. He had presently come back to them, to say with his customary smooth languor—

"I am *so* sorry, don't you know. A dear old frriend of mine—poor fellow!—he has had grreat misfortunes; and here *figurez vous?*—here! he is verry badly trreated. If you will excuse me a minute?"

A few seconds later, they had a glimpse of him in perspective through the open door, twirling his moustache, while he held a button of the proprietor's coat and talked to him evidently for his good. The only words that faintly reached their ears sounded suspiciously like—"damned scoundrrel, don't you know?"

He rejoined them, perfectly suave and apologetic, finished his coffee with an air of exhaustion, and paid the bill. As they left the room the proprietor bowed before them low and obsequious. And yet, if a cabman drove over his toes, or a crossing-sweeper bespattered him with mud, the chances were that he would apologise to them for being in the way.

Jocelyn had a much kindlier feeling for him than she had had in the old days. His companionship took her out of herself. She brooded less, regained much of her spirits. She could not shake off the feeling of being alone, of being lost in a forest of uncompanionable trees, but the fear became more shadowy—less substantial.

They went about a good deal by themselves. Jocelyn had always been, both by nature and education, unconventional in such matters, and now a kind of recklessness possessed her. Mrs. Travis indeed had a high sense of the proprieties, but she had a higher sense of comfort; she did not care at all for music or pictures, not much for theatres, so she contented herself and salved her conscience with those entertainments where one ate.

As for Nielsen, he had expanded with prosperity. In his relations with Jocelyn, he seemed to have more time, no longer any reason to cramp his emotions into a small space. He found it pleasant to play with the sensation of being alone in the field—with a newly-born feeling of comradeship. Also, he was always beset with a sense of enigma, of something in the girl which had not formerly been there—in an impersonal sort of way he felt he would like to find out what it was; just as, when he was a small boy, he had cut open his toys to see what was inside. It would have been wrong to say he was not in love with her, he was—but the attitude of his mind was leisurely.

One day they were driving down Sloane Street on their way to a theatre. At the edge of the pavement, as they passed, a shop assistant in an apron and grey flannel shirt sleeves was twirling a red-bristled mop. If his life had depended on it, his puckered visage could not have expressed a more concentrated emotion. Jocelyn plucked Nielsen's sleeve: "Look what a limited thing the human face is!" she said, with a sudden little shiver. "If that man had committed a murder he couldn't look more dreadful, and he's only twisting a mop!" The hansom whirled close past the man with the sound of frequent hoofs and jingled bell, and Nielsen only had a glimpse of a momentarily suspended mop, and a pale, expressionless visage. Having missed the effect, he looked at his companion's face instead as she leaned forward in the cab. It was very white, and the brows were drawn together as if she were in sudden pain. He had a gleam of recollection, and for the first time since seeing her again, all the old, painful sense of a barrier between them.

Jocelyn looked at him.

"Ah!" she said, with sudden inspiration, "you are thinking you would like to read my thoughts, to know what's behind the mask, but you never will, you see. We're all alone—always alone—aren't we?"

She spoke quietly enough, rather like a child asking for information, but somehow he had the impression that she was frightened. He put one of his gloved hands soothingly upon hers. It was the first time he had touched her except in the exchange of ordinary greeting, and he was surprised and confused by the sudden vehemence with which she snatched her hand away, and folding her arms, leant back in her corner of the cab, almost as if he had struck her.

He said nothing—he had nothing to say. She was as gentle and friendly to him as usual all the rest of the afternoon.

Chapter Twenty-one

UPON one Sunday afternoon a few weeks later, Jocelyn made an expedition with Nielsen to Watts's Studio in the Melbury Road. It was one of the last days of April. There was a soft grey sky, lit every now and then with watery gleams of sun. They walked across Kensington Gardens, where the trees were full of young, green foliage, and the earth damp with the last of April showers. The birds were calling all round them.

Jocelyn was in one of her most vivid moods. As was usual with her when in high spirits, words rippled from her lips in a way quite irresponsible and very charming. She walked briskly with a springing step, as straight as a dart, her small head thrown slightly back between her shoulders, her eyes dancing and a smile on her lips. She always dressed in a manner peculiar to her own desires, yet she never seemed behind the times—a problem for analytical dressmakers. To-day she had had the whim to put on a black dress, with some creamy lace round the neck and in the front of the bodice. Thus attired and with a black hat, she appealed irresistibly to Nielsen's sense of the fitness of things. Her small face seemed to gleam out of its black and white setting like a jewel. He squared his figure as he walked, and held his head up with a feeling of pride.

In the Studio groups of people stood, in a subdued light, discussing the pictures in low tones. The spirit of allegory stared out upon them from the walls. Imagination laid a spell upon the eye, and upon the tongue. Jocelyn's face had become suddenly grave and earnest. The brilliancy went out of her brown eyes, they grew profound, dark, and reverent; her impressionable, artistic nature was at once under the master's influence. She did not, indeed, lose her sense of criticism, her discrimination, but she seemed to have become in immediate sympathy with the painter's views and aims, judging him, as it were, from his own standpoint. Nielsen, on the other hand, though by no means unimpressed, retained his own point of view. With his head a little upon one side, and his hand caressing his moustache, he appeared to discuss with himself the merits of each picture in an adjusted see-saw of *pro* and *con*. For a few minutes they became separated, and when Nielsen came back to her side, he found her standing before the wonderful picture of Paolo and Francesca. Her hands were clasped in front of her, her face was very still, and there were tears in her eyes.

Nielsen said nothing, but stood and looked at the picture too.

He had never seen it before. The tragedy in it arrested him—the measureless tragedy of that man and woman whirled through space in the resistless rush of a linked unrest—the unspeakable, compassionate anguish on the man's lips, the undying love in his shadowed eyes, the suffering, and the eternal, wistful faith of the woman's face. If ever the truth of life has been revealed in art, surely it is in that picture. There, is all the joy of life, and all its suffering, endless motion, and triumphant love.

Nielsen experienced a kind of indignation—it was unpleasantly disturbing. He swallowed a lump in his throat and turned away abruptly, he did not care to look at it too long. It was a relief to hear a man behind him remark to a woman that the "glass" was going down. After all, those were the things that mattered, luckily, more than a hundred dismal pictures. The "glass" was going down! That was infinitely satisfactory. He put his hands into the pockets of his overcoat, and worked them gently up and down. He felt much better. Then he wiped his eyeglass, and looked at Jocelyn.

She was still standing in front of the picture, looking as if she were going to faint. All his indignation returned. He went and got her a chair, put it down with its back to the picture, and made her sit in it. His eyes glowed angrily, and he twisted his moustache fiercely. Then he expressed his feelings—

'I should like to get that Monsieur Watts, and hang him on the walls of his own studio as a—a—pr-recept." When he had caught the word, he hissed it from under his moustache.

"I consider it is quite indecent, don't you know—the—the—confounded picture has made you ill."

A rush of colour had come into Jocelyn's cheeks, and, as she got up from her chair, she said—

"It's very stupid of me! Don't abuse the picture, please, I love it. It's only coming into this hot room after the walk. I'm all right now." She insisted on going round the studio again, and even upon discussing the merits of the various pictures, but they both avoided the "Paolo and Francesca," and Nielsen knew by the tone of her voice that she was not herself.

On the way home in a cab, she hardly spoke at all, and leant back gazing straight in front of her. Nielsen became garrulous; he did not in the least understand what was the matter, but he considerately wished by chatter to divert her thoughts.

"Prrogress, civilisation!" he said, spreading his fingers out of the cab into an inattentive space, and bending forward with puckered eyes, "Ah! The 'artist!' He is nowhere. It is all 'the man of action,' don't you know. He leads the way—he is the cause. The other fellow is only the effect, you see; he exists because there is somebody there already to hold him out his brread and butter. Lōōk at the Romans! Ah! There you have the rreal Philistine. But lōōk at his civilisation; lōōk at his rroads, lōōk at his baths, he—washed! They were men of action, and they held the brread and butter in their hands, don't you know, for the other fellows to come and eat. Lōōk at this country! Here you have more frreedom, more comfort, more justice than anywhere else that I have been; and yet you are barbarous men of action, don't you know. Not one in a hundred of you has any sense of form or colour, but you manage to have as much art and as much music and literature, on the whole, as any other country. It is all a case of brread and butter, you see. You can pay the—how do you say it—the piper, so you call the tune."

Jocelyn shook her head gently and said, "There are two sides to that."

"Certainly, my dear young lady, there are two sides to every question. I am quite willing to hear the other side—but to me music—pictures—books, they are all frrills, charrming frrills. They don't begin till the garment is completed. They rrise out of leisure, and there is *not* any leisure, don't you see, until there is alrready a

132

civilisation. After all, a man must eat—that comes first." He nodded his head mournfully, as if the fact were painful to him.

But all his efforts to draw her into argument were of no avail; the drive ended silently, and he left her at the door of the Mansions. He walked away slowly eastwards, looking absently at the grey water running through the dark arches of the bridge, and every now and then shaking his head gravely.

Jocelyn climbed the two flights of stairs to the flat, and let herself in with her key. She went straight to her bedroom, the thought of her aunt's society at that moment was intolerable to her, and she muffled her footsteps as she passed the drawing-room.

She took off her hat and gloves, and flung herself into a chair in front of the empty fireplace. She sat there for some minutes, rocking herself to and fro, with her hands crossed in her lap.

She was haunted by that picture, its endless whirlwind of motion, its anguish. In the face of Paolo something reminded her of Giles. It seemed to her that she read in the picture, for herself and for him, the cruel denial of rest, the resistless decree of an eternal punishment through immeasurable space.

She sprang to her feet, and paced to and fro the length of her room, pressing her hands to her throbbing temples. After a time, the soft monotony of her own footsteps on the carpet soothed her; she paused in front of the window, and flung it open. The air was sweet and warm, and there was a faint sound of raindrops plashing gently on the young leaves of the trees. The church clock was striking "five." She shut her eyes and listened—another and another echoed the refrain, till the world seemed full of a wistful chiming. It ceased. She reached her hand out along the window, leaning against the half-opened casement. Some drops of rain fell upon her face.

The paroxysm of her pain had passed away, she only felt alone —very tired, and alone.

Presently she bathed her face with cold water, changed her dress, and went to the drawing-room pale and quite calm.

Mrs. Travis, upright in her chair, with watchful green eyes and a silver-grey dress, was playing "Patience." Jocelyn shivered a little.

Chapter Twenty-two

UPON the same Sunday afternoon, in a small port on the eastern Spanish seaboard, Giles Legard leant over the rail of a long, forlorn-looking, wooden jetty. Against the black piles which upheld it the sea heaved inwards in smooth ripples. Every now and then wisps of dark seaweed floated by, and up the sides of the piles the green slime gleamed in the hot sunshine. Keeping a precarious foothold on the slippery cross-beams with his bare, brown feet, a red-capped fisher boy plucked mussels, dropping them into a basket slung on his arm. The sea, hushed and bright, stretched past the jetty to the town, which rose in compact white tiers under the lee of a sandy waste of hills; on the hard line of the eastern horizon the dim haze of an island was visible.

A brig, with sails set, was sidling out of the harbour against a head wind. A row of fishermen and loafers, barelegged or booted, with swarthy faces, and blue clothing, came running down the jetty, stretching a tow-rope hove to them from the brig, and shouting in a babel of uncouth words. Legard, with his hands in his pockets, and his cap drawn over his eyes, turned his back against the rail, and watched them idly.

They strained on the rope, laughing and talking in a strange medley of words and dialects. Then, as if by consent, they ceased hauling, and paused in relaxed attitudes, shouting irrelevantly at the brig a jumble of foreign words. A bearded man, in a peaked cap, standing on the poop, put his hand to his mouth, and the hail came with a steady ring over the water, "Pūlley! Haūley!"

The words had an inflection, as of a man speaking to children, a kind of compassionate superiority. The chain of men strained forward again upon the rope, and, with a clatter of feet and voices, went surging up the pier.

"Pulley! Hauley!" Words comprehended of every nation under the sun, words by the aid of which men make shift to go through the business of life. They struck a chord in Legard's heart that had not sounded for many years. They roused in him a longing for action, and a feeling of pride, such as one has when one reads of some gallant feat done by a countryman. He watched the Union Jack stream out in the wind as the brig cleared the end of the jetty with a queer feeling, that made him shuffle his feet on the tarred boards, and swear softly to himself. Then he took out a cigar, and bit the end very hard, looking into the distance over the sea.

The men, broken up now into groups, lolled on the jetty sides, or lounged back up the pier talking and spitting. They looked at him as they passed, with dark eyes, curious or indifferent, and exchanged remarks in low voices. He was a strange bird to them; an English traveller did not often find his way to their town.

Gradually, under the brassy sun, the jetty resumed its look of desolation.

Giles took his cap off, and wiped his forehead. His face, which was tanned a deep sallow brown, had somewhat hardened and set; the features looked as if always held in a vice of constraint. There was no trace of the old languor in his eyes, they looked up clear and straight from under his brows, but they had a rather wistful expression, as if always seeking for something. His dark hair had grown very grey at the sides of his head and on his temples. In his thin flannel suit his tall figure looked lean to emaciation, but his muscles, from constant hard exercise, were like whipcord. He had that day returned to the town, whence he had started a month before on a restless wander through a wild part of Spain.

He replaced his cap, and began to pace uneasily up and down the jetty, stopping every now and then to take a long look under his hand towards the town. He muttered to himself at intervals. He had begun rather to have the habit of talking to himself—a habit which tells of much loneliness. . . .

The test of a man's temperament is the way in which he manages himself under trouble. Legard had managed himself in solitude. A hundred times in those ten months he had been impelled to seek distraction in society, dissipation, excitement—to try and forget, for it was his nature to fly from pain; but something in him had always revolted at the last moment, and he had shrunk back. He had, deeply rooted, the feeling that if he even *tried* to rid himself of his suffering and his desolation, he would lose loyalty, the one thing which remained to him. If he gave that up, he felt that he must go under—irretrievably under. It was not choice so much as instinct that compelled him to hold on to his bitter, regretful longing; and with his grip fast on *that* plank, he felt his head still above water. Of the memory of his wife's death he tried not to be mindful. At times a sudden spasm of self-loathing and of superstitious horror caught him, as it were, by the throat, but there was a certain gravity in his mind which helped him—the ballast of his own egotism, his matter-of-fact conviction of the futility of regret, and his feeling for what was of use in the future. That same feeling of loyalty, to which he clung so tenaciously, blunted, even at times negatived, the bite of remorse. It became a sort of painful pleasure to him to reason the thing out with a grim analysis. The evil did not seem to him to lie in the wrong he had done to the woman he loved, nor in the guilty inaction by which he had sought to repair that wrong, it lay further back, in the fibre of his own nature and the infirmity of his will—he felt that he had suffered for it, was always suffering. If repentance be suffering—he repented; if it be knowledge of self—he repented, for he was getting to know his own limitations as he had never known them before; but if it be that feeling which says, "Give me the past again, that I may act otherwise!" he did not repent, for he was not sure that he would act differently. The thing was over and done with, he had behaved like a coward and a scoundrel, but regret was of no use—he looked to the future, to the time, if it ever came, when he should see Jocelyn again; and in long reveries over smoky camp fires, on the decks of ships under starry skies, beneath the burning sun of the desert, and the unfallen snow-clouds of mountains, his face became gradually and indelibly stamped with that drawn expression of constraint. He had wandered about unceasingly, in the Austrian highlands, in Turkey, Algeria, Spain, anywhere, indeed, where he could get hard physical exertion, and be unlikely to meet people. He would have gone to the East, or to South Africa, but he would not put himself out of reach of his letters. Time would surely have done more for him, if he would have cut himself completely adrift, but he would not. Every month he received a letter from Jocelyn; it was never anything but a bare record of doings, smelling of violets, scanty and formal, and very precious to him. It began without any prefix, ended simply "Jocelyn"—it would be hard to say the amount of comfort he derived from that solitary and dumb confession of a link between them. . . .

At this moment, as he strode across and across the jetty gnawing his moustache, the cigar, still unlit, between his fingers, he was waiting for Jacopo's return from the post-office. It was nine weeks since he had received a letter, and even *he* had not realised how much they meant to him, till they had ceased to come. He had put off the day of his return to the coast, in sheer dread of not getting one, and now he had not had the courage to go and see for himself. He felt sick with suspense. He threw away his cigar unsmoked. Two seagulls swooped on it, shrilling discordantly. A faint, muffled sound of voices came down to him from a group of men and women at the far end of the jetty, and the salt wind fanned his cheek gently. He gazed towards the shore, where the world seemed to stand still in hot, hard lines.

A figure presently detached itself at the end of the jetty, and came towards him. He recognised Jacopo by his light clothes and wide-brimmed hat, and by the dog with him.

He forced himself to stand still and wait, his hands crossed behind his back, his limbs and every feature of his face quivering with the strain of repression. He was thinking: supposing there were no letter!—what then? There *must* be one!

Jacopo was walking fast. In the same breath he seemed to Giles to be years arriving, and to come with the swiftness of a wind. When he was within fifty yards the boy's hand went to his pocket, and the dog, breaking from him, ran to his master and thrust his pointed nose up against his legs.

In spite of himself he turned away, grasped the jetty rail hard, and stood, looking with eyes that saw nothing, at the horizon.

Jacopo came up to him, cool and silent.

"Well?" said Giles without turning.

"There are letters, Signore—three."

Still leaning over the rail, Legard put out his hand, his fingers closed on the letters, and he said—

"Thank you, Jacopo, you have been rather long." He spoke with the idea of gaining time.

"*Si, Signore*, the man at the post was very stupid."

"You are sure these are all?"

"*Si, Signore*, sure."

"Thank you, wait at the end of the pier till I call you."

Jacopo moved away; Giles, clutching the letters, looked blankly after his retreating figure. Shikari rubbed a wet nose suddenly against his hand, and then stretched his body at full length, placing his forepaws on the rail, and working his nostrils from side to side with a snuffle at the unconscious sea. Giles bit his lips, raised his hand quickly, and without glancing at the outsides tore open the letters one by one. He dropped them unread into his pocket, lifted his cap, and ran his hand through his hair.

Nothing! He took a rapid turn across the jetty and back again, followed solemnly by the dog. Nothing! He muttered to himself one or two commonplaces. "Very awkward thing! Odd! Very odd!" Words absolutely inexpressive of his feelings, but somehow comforting.

He took Shikari's forepaws, and drew them on to his chest, put them down again, and took another turn across the jetty. He stood, and looked out on the other side, and said, "My God!" in a low voice. He drew another cigar out of his case, lit it, and put it back again.

Nothing. Nine weeks! She had ceased to write! What did it mean? Was she ill?

He called suddenly "Jacopo!"

The boy came quickly, his slight figure in its nankeen suit, at once alert and watchful.

"Go, and find out when there is a train to join the main line for England. Get a carriage and horses; have the things ready —we shall start for it at the earliest minute, do you understand?"

"*Si, Signore!*" The boy whistled to Shikari, and vanished down the pier at a long stealthy trot.

Giles crammed his cap down over his eyes, as if he were riding at a fence, and shut his teeth together with a snap. He *must* act! He *must* know. Phew! That was a relief. He twisted the slight ends of his dark moustache fiercely upwards, and took a glance all round him.

Westwards the brig's sails were glistening under the sun like the snow of a mountain peak.

Thrusting his hands into the pockets of his coat he walked rapidly down the pier.

Chapter Twenty-three

TRAVELLING night and day, Legard arrived in London late on Wednesday afternoon. Except upon one occasion, for a few days, he had not been in England for twelve years. It was strange to him that every one should talk his own language; the feel of the air, the grey irregular streets, the soberness of costume were strange. He drove straight to the Langham Hotel. He had a friendly recollection of it from days when he used to come up from Eton and stop there with his mother to see the match at Lord's. It was very much the same, inside and out—quite immutable apparently—only it seemed to him, like everything else, exceedingly dingy.

After he had seen to the necessities of his servant and his dog, he dined; and when he came out into the hall it was already nine o'clock. He lit a cigar, but he found it quite impossible to sit and smoke it quietly. He was very tired from his long journey, but he could not sit still. He was possessed by that feeling of restlessness which haunts one who has come a long way for a certain purpose, and finds at the end a gap of inaction intervening. He walked out of the hotel, and stood on the pavement staring blankly up the lighted avenue of Portland Place.

The restless roar of traffic from Regent Street attracted him, it was companionable—it suited his mood. He began to walk slowly towards it. The warm air was full of the smell of tobacco smoke and patchouli, and of other odours. On either hand of the street the lamps sent forth shafts of white or golden light upon the constant streams of passengers, motley and white-faced, who thronged the pavements. The curve of the quadrant bent in a clear-cut line against the impalpable loom of the purple heavens; and, through the streets, the traffic ran like blood through the veins of a strong man.

Giles walked on slowly, smoking. The electricity in the air, the intense stir of life around him, made upon his tired and unaccustomed faculties a profound impression. He felt benumbed, like a man in a nightmare. At Piccadilly Circus he stopped, and stood, staring about him. A brake filled with a pleasure party passed close. Girls leaning out of it swung in their hands coloured lanterns, which lit up their flushed faces and disordered hair. It was gone in a medley of song-snatches, rattling hoofs, empty laughter, and twinkling lights. A string of policemen filed by, solemn and bulky, each one a ridiculous embodiment of the earnestness of life. Out of the blare and turmoil of the street a fire-engine charged towards him, swaying from side to side, with the thunder of wheels and a harsh incessant shouting.

As he stood there a woman touched him on the arm and leered up at him; some one blew a whiff of tobacco in his face; black-hatted, shiny-booted men languidly held the pavement with gingerly steps; in front of him the coloured letters of an advertisement went in and out; newspaper men, like ghouls battening meagrely upon the misfortunes of other people, yelled dismally; and the bells of cabs and bicycles sounded swiftly, vanishing into chaos on this side and that. Coming after the silence of lonely places, it was strange. Every one had something to do, and was doing it with solemn fury; even the drunken man lurching at the gutter was earnestly drunk. It was curious after the south; yet instinctively, and without thinking about it, he understood it very well, much better than all that he had lived with for so many years. At this moment, with nothing to do but wait, kill time, and deaden the suspense in his mind, he was waiting very earnestly. He was of the same blood and the same grain as all that mass of humanity around him, which surged ceaselessly to and fro upon its business.

With an effort he roused himself, and made his way across Piccadilly. He formed the resolution, suddenly, to put an end to his suspense. It would be too late to see Jocelyn in any event, but he could at least find out something about her, where she was, perhaps how she was. At all events it would kill some time. He chose the slowest means of progression, and climbed on to a

Chelsea omnibus. He sat in front, leaning forward, with his long legs drawn back under the seat, his shoulders high and square, and his soft felt hat covering his forehead. As the 'bus rumbled along Piccadilly in the stream of the traffic, past a narrow red streak of stationed cab lights and the overhanging trees of the Green Park, the driver, a man with a permanent cold, looked round at him curiously. The tanned, drawn face, with its thin, black moustache above the set jaw, had a queer look to his insular eyes. He would have volunteered remarks, but, as he afterwards observed hoarsely to his mate—

"That furrin' lookin' gent as sat be'ind o' me lawst trip 'ad a mug on 'im as dried the words in yer mouth. Looked as if 'e were kind o' settin' on 'ot bricks, 'e did, and knowed it too; a rum bird 'e was."

"Right," returned the mate, a cockney, " 'e was English, though —asked me the w'y to Cheeyne Walk an' giv' me a bob—quite the gent—there ain't too many of 'is sort abaout."

"Oh! ay! A right eno' gent—'igher rup!"

When Giles reached the Mansions he hesitated for some minutes before he found the courage to go in. At the sound of his footsteps upon the tiled floor, the porter, a large personage in blue, with a stolid red face, and an evening paper in his hand, appeared from a corner and stood under the hanging lamp, an illuminated image of matter-of-fact civility.

"What name, sir?" He had a voice that leapt out of him with unexpected brevity, and a habit of twitching one eyelid.

Giles felt suddenly cool, and unemotional, with the calmness peculiar to nervous organisations in critical moments.

"Does Mrs. Travis live here?" he said.

"Yes, sir, number three."

"And, Miss Ley?"

"Yes, sir, same number."

"Ah!" He gave his moustache a twist, but he was not conscious of any particular feeling of relief, or indeed of any feeling except a slight surprise at himself.

"The ladies are well, I hope?"

"Quite well, thank'ee, sir. Do you wish me to send up your name?"

"No, thank you—er—that is—I should like to write a note. Can you give me a sheet of paper and an envelope?"

"Cert'nly, sir." The porter, disappearing into a decorative sentry-box, emerged with pen and paper. He set them down upon a table. Giles wrote these words upon a sheet of paper: —"Langham Hotel, Wednesday—May I come and see you to-morrow at 4 o'clock? G.L." folded it, closed it in an envelope, and addressed it, "Miss Jocelyn Ley." Then he stood, and looked at the porter, whose eyelid went up and down with regularity, giving the impression that he was continually endeavouring to relieve the stolidity of his visage with a wink.

"You will see Miss Ley to-morrow morning?"

"I can see her, if you wish, sir."

"Give her this, not to-night, you understand, to-morrow morning."

"Yes, sir."

"Here's something for your trouble." He pulled out a coin, handed it to the porter, and turned on his heel. The porter's voice pursued him abruptly.

"Beg y'r pardon, sir, you giv' me a sov'reign, sir."

"Oh! did I? All right!"

The rustling in the trees outside was refreshing, the river consolingly dark and profound. He muttered irrelevantly to himself: "Here endeth the first lesson," and leant against the stone parapet of the embankment, looking at the rows of lighted windows, and wondering which was hers. The dark figure of the porter, legs apart, was still outlined in the lighted cave of the open doorway. With a feeling of being "moved on," Giles set his face eastwards by the side of the quiet river. Over the busy part of the town the dark vault of the sky was powdered with innumerable gold specks, and there was a hum, as of gigantic insects, in the air. He walked a few paces, and became suddenly conscious of the fact that he was dog-tired. Hailing a hansom he drove home in it, more than half asleep.

When he came out of the hotel the next day, a bright sun was staining wet patches of the pavement a ruddy orange, the air was clear, and the streets had a freshly-washed appearance. He had some matters of business to attend to, and he forced himself to go about them. He found nevertheless, in the afternoon, that he was at the Mansions fully half-an-hour too soon, and he paced restlessly backwards and forwards along the embankment until the appointed time.

Chapter Twenty-four

WHEN four o'clock sounded at last, he walked into the hall of the Mansions. As he mounted the stairs his sensations were not enviable.

Would she be in? Would she see him? Alone? He felt that he would almost rather not see her at all than in the presence of other people. His heart beat till he felt sick, and he paused for some minutes, outside the door, before ringing the bell.

"Is Miss Ley at home?"

The maid, a rosy-cheeked damsel with a fresh and wholesome face, answered, "Yes, sir."

He felt dismay and intense relief at the same moment. He pulled himself together with an effort, and followed her.

"What name, sir?"

"Legard."

The door was thrown open, and he heard his name pronounced into a room which he could scarcely see from a feeling of giddiness that came over him. The door closed behind. There was a faint scent of violets, and he was conscious of the rustle of a skirt. He stood within the room twisting his moustache, and staring about him with uncertain eyes. Jocelyn had risen from a chair near the window. He took a step forward and stopped. Her face was white, then crimson, then white again; her hands gripped the back of the chair from which she had risen. Neither offered to move, or to speak; they stood still, and looked fixedly at each other, an unsparing space of conventional carpet between them.

After the first sign of emotion, Jocelyn's face wore a mask of discouragement. It showed dark and mysterious against the bright sunlight behind her, and reproach seemed to be looking out of her eyes. Giles, clutching the fold of his coat across his chest, gazed at her with a countenance from which hunger had suddenly driven every other emotion.

Jocelyn spoke, and her voice sounded dull and expressionless. "Why?" she said. "What was the good?"

Giles involuntarily took a half-step forward.

"Why?" he repeated. "Why? You stopped writing—I didn't know—how could I——"

"Didn't I write long enough?" she said wearily. "It didn't seem any use going on. I wanted to forget. I didn't know where you were —you might have been dead." A sudden ring of irritability, telling of shaken nerves, came into the tone of her voice. Giles had a swift sense of injustice; he remembered the misery it had cost him not to answer those letters.

"I obeyed you, I would have given the world to write."

"You should have gone on obeying me. Why have you come back? Why?" She spoke as if under the spur of some unbearable thought. She stamped her foot on the soft carpet, and her dark eyes were full of resentment. Giles winced, his head dropped upon his chest. This was the other side of the question; she made him feel guilty of an act of brutality. He asked himself why he had come back to torture her? Because he, a strong man, could not bear pain! The poorness of the reason struck him for the first time. As always, he admitted the other side at its full value without question.

"I love you," was all he found to say.

"You love me! But you don't care how you hurt me." She pressed her lips tightly together. He could not help the swift thought, "She is cruel," and hated himself for it in the same breath. He put his clenched hands against his forehead, and the words escaped him—

"Is that all? *All*—after——"

"What more do you want? What more do you expect?"

He gazed long and fixedly at her with the searching, upward look in his eyes peculiar to them. He could see nothing behind the mask of her resentful face. It fixed a barrier between them—impenetrable. Through the half-open window a puff of wind strayed in, and the petals of some flowers upon the table stirred; he heard the sheets of the open music on the piano rustling, and the clock ticking very solemnly. During a moment of numbness he had no other sensation. Then his mind leaped suddenly back to painful consciousness. How beautiful she was; standing, slender and motionless, between him and the light! How pitiless! So! It was all over! He had only exchanged the uncertainty of misery for the certainty of it! He made a movement with his mouth, a movement of dumb pain, and in the spasmodic motion which intolerable suffering exacts, strode past her to the window, and stood there, with his back to her, and his hands over his eyes. He tried to reason. "After all," he thought, "a man has some pride—I'd better get away." The subtle fragrance in the room tortured his senses—her fragrance. He stood motionless while long seconds crept by, and found—that he had no pride. He suffered so keenly that his reason refused to come to his aid. He could not think of the why or the wherefore of anything, of what it meant or did not mean; he could *only* feel; and he seemed to have no tongue with which to plead for himself. It was all over! He choked back a sob rising in his throat. . . .

He had not heard any movement in the room, but he suddenly felt fingers pulling at his hands. Jocelyn was standing beside him, looking at him with pitying and mournful eyes.

"Don't!" she said, "don't grieve so! I'm not worth it."

He knelt down, and clasping her knees looked up at her. She put a hand over her eyes, with a soft movement.

"I'm not worth it," she repeated.

Suddenly his tongue was loosed, a pent-up torrent of tender words forced its way between his dry lips. He kissed her hands and her dress convulsively. She stood for a moment submitting, shivering a little, a faint colour in her cheeks, then she cried brokenly—

"Oh, get up! *Get* up, don't kneel to me. How *can* you—when I am—what I am?" and burst into a passion of sobbing. The sense of degradation vivid in her voice wounded him like the cut of a knife. He sprang to his feet, and took her in his arms. He was quite silent, but his lips trembled. She grew quiet at last, till only little shudders running through her body, pressed against his own, told him of her emotion. They stood together at the window. In the momentary lull of his feeling, he had dim impressions of outward things—of the blue sky and the shifting play of white clouds, of the river dancing through the green of the trees in glittering patches. At intervals the melodious and doleful cry of a costermonger came to his ears through the soft air, the air that was young with the fluttering of leaves and the chirping of birds.

The spirit of the day seemed to be calling with a whisper of invitation. He felt a sudden hope spring up in his heart. Could her love be dead? He put his lips down to the level of her bent head—

"Have you *no* love for me, Jocelyn?" he said.

She did not answer, but bent her head a little lower, and he felt a faint pressure of her fingers upon his hand, a momentary clinging which passed, and left them cold and lifeless in his grasp. She *did* love him still! He felt it with a great joy. Was it possible then that she could throw away everything that made life bright, that gave it form, and colour, and meaning? And for what? For a shadow! Because of a memory. The matter-of-fact temper of his mind revolted. For a shadow! After all, nothing more!

His eyes fell upon the gleaming river.

"Come away from it all, my darling. Be my wife. Let me take you somewhere where you can forget. If you only *will,* you *can.* The world is so beautiful; I will give you everything. Won't you come?" and he raised his eyes to her face. There were the marks of tears upon it, and her hands moved with a little gesture of helplessness as though she found life too heavy for her. She shook her head wearily.

"Why?" he said, seizing her hands, so that she had to turn towards him. "Why?"

She did not answer at once, and when she did, every word went through him.

"You want me to take *her* place, and you say, forget? How could I? Forget! In *her place. Ah!* don't ask me!"

From the living pain in her voice, he had a gleam of insight that to her the shadow was substance, the substance only shadows, and he said in a voice that shook, in spite of all his efforts to keep it calm and persuasive—

"Think, darling, can it be *worse* together than alone? Won't you think of *me* a little?" He wanted to break into passionate words telling of his starvation, but somehow he couldn't; they refused to come, they rose indeed to his lips, but vanished ashamed and unspoken.

"Think of you? I *do* think of you. Do you think I don't know, that I haven't thought and thought? I can't trust myself. I should

147

only make you wretched—I'm not good enough. It's too strong for me—I can't forget. I'm not good enough. Can't you see what it is you're asking of me?"

His grasp tightened upon her hands. In spite of himself he did see her side of the question, something of what it meant to her proud and sensitive nature to stand in the place of the dead woman; it did not move his passionate desire by the breadth of one single hair, but it deprived him suddenly of the power of fighting her with words. He seemed to see beforehand all her answers to his arguments, all the pitiless irony of the situation. It was not *in* him to thrust his convictions down the throats of other people. He wished to, but he was not able. The fatal turn of his mind was always to see the other view. He could only say—

"For *my* sake, dear."

"It can't be—it can't be; it would kill me, perhaps both of us. I now what would come. *Her* place! Horrible!" She shivered as if with deadly cold, and shut her eyes. Then she said quite calmly—

"Some day, you see, it would be too strong for me, I should leave you, or kill myself. I can't love as you do; if I could, perhaps it would be different. I know myself, I'm shallow, not good enough for you."

In the expression of her face fear, pity, and wounded pride were strangely blended, and her voice was measured and even. He had an immense inclination to break into harsh laughter. Not good enough for him! What a reason! It was as if some one, holding a cup of water to the lips of a man dying of thirst, had snatched it away, with the words, "Don't drink, it is not cold enough."

He repeated the words—

"Not good enough!" In his desperation he turned away from her, and walked up and down the room.

"So!" burst from him suddenly and very bitterly, "it was only an episode! All our pain, all my life, all yours, for it *is* all yours, I tell you—only an episode!" It was the only harsh thing he had ever said to her—a betrayal of his inmost instinct—a treachery to his nature. He knew it; and dropping into a chair, rested his head in his hands, muttering, "Forgive me."

There was a tense silence in the room . . . Jocelyn came quickly from the window. She sank upon her knees at his side.

"I can't !" she sobbed. "I would—but oh! I can't. *Anything* but that!" and she pressed her face against him.

"Not that, dearest! I *will* be anything else to you—*anything*. I love you! But not that—oh! *not* that."

What was she saying? The blood throbbed in his veins; the perfume of her breath was on his cheek, he could feel the warmth of her body against his knee. The whole vehemence of his passion stirred within him. The temptation was such that he writhed; his senses reeled with the desire to gain, and lose, all things in her embrace. His instinct told him it was ruin for him and for her, but what did it matter? . . . He threw his arms round her. She rubbed her cheek against his hand with a little tender movement, and he felt it suddenly wet. A pure and great pity took hold of him. "God help me!" he thought. "Not again!" He got up on to his feet, and raised her, smoothing the loosened hair back from her temples.

"No, no!' he said gently. "No, *no!* Anything rather——"

He felt he was talking to himself, not to her, that he was suddenly thrust back into utter isolation; and he knew that he must get away quickly before the maddened throbbing in his blood over-mastered him.

"This will make you ill, sweet," he said, "I had better go—yes —I'll write. God bless you! Good-bye!"

He did not know how he got out of the room, how he left her, or where. Everything swam in a mist before his eyes, but at last he found himself on the stairs, going down slowly and deliberately, and trying to pull his gloves on to his hands. A man passed him at the foot of the stairs, and stopped in his ascent to look after him.

Chapter Twenty-five

GILES stepped outside, and turned indifferently to the left. A few paces down the street was a public-house, he turned into it, and calling for a glass of brandy drank it off at a gulp. As he was coming out a man touched him smartly on the shoulder from behind. He turned round, and saw Nielsen. He was panting slightly from emotion or haste, his eyes had a red and angry look, and he planted his square figure firmly on the pavement in front of Legard.

"Look here, you know," he said, "this will not do, this is not the thing, you know, Monsieur Legard"—the words tumbled over each other grotesquely in his anger: *"C'est une lâcheté vous savez, c' que vous avez fait là."*

"What?" said Giles; he stood with clenched hands before the other, and his face was set and savage-looking.

"This, what you have done to Miss Ley, to that angel. What is it you have said to her to make her cry? *Pardieu! C'est un peu trop fort."*

Giles's face quivered at the words, then was instantly hard again. He looked at the other, with his jaw thrust forward.

"What is it to you?" he said.

He felt grateful for the sensation of anger. By nature very gentle, at this moment he felt a savage enjoyment.

"You have hurt her, I will not have it; do you understand me, you—you?"

"Ah!" said Giles, and he looked very dangerous. Each man

felt that all the old antagonism between them was being compressed into the few words they spoke.

Nielsen continued, tugging at his moustache, his face white with anger.

"What you have done you shall not again do; I will take care of it—*I.* You are not fit to speak to her, *vous êtes un lâche, vous avez tué votr' femme!*" The last words seemed to explode in his mouth before they found vent—he had probably never intended to utter them.

Giles did not move, he only gritted his teeth together.

"Perhaps!" he said between them. At the word, so measured and so strange, Nielsen's hands dropped inertly to his sides, his face expressed a sudden blank amazement, all his anger seemed to evaporate in surprise. A barrel organ was playing within a few feet of where they stood, the man, as he turned the dismal handle, grinned and kept holding a greasy hat towards them.

Giles, taking a step forward, spoke in a low voice—

"Look here, Mr. Nielsen," he said, "I don't take this sort of thing from you or any other man. Get out of my way, please, or by God, I'll throw you."

He stepped past Nielsen, who involuntarily moved to one side, and made no attempt to detain him. His face still expressed a blank astonishment, and he was endeavouring to fix his eyeglass into his eye as a short-sighted man does when he is puzzled. Giles strode along. The organ-grinder muttered: "*Buon giorno, Signore,*" thrusting his hat almost into his face, an intruding triviality which was quite acceptable to him.

He walked quickly eastwards. The incident with Nielsen had, for the moment, done him good; he thought grimly of the sudden change which had come over the Swede's broad face. It served as a temporary distraction to his thoughts. But the next instant he was pursued again by a dull sense of utter unhappiness. Twice he actually turned round, and began to retrace his steps towards the Mansions, and each time his mind in the end was bent against it by the feeling, light and unsubstantial as a feather, that it would be ridiculous to go back now. He knew that it formed no part of the real balancing of his reasons, for or against, but there it was, a chance surface feeling just sufficient to turn the scale. He thought too of Nielsen, with a sensation of jealousy—which he knew all the time to be unreal. What was he doing there? What did his interference mean? He tried to bring the feeling to his own support, but it slipped away from him with the memory of the words Jocelyn had spoken. "I love you—I will be anything to you, *anything* but that——"

He got back to his hotel at last, having formed and reformed resolutions a dozen times. He drank some more brandy. He felt so miserable that he thought he could understand the Canadian Indian, who will drink red ink because it gives him a feeling of warmth inside. A benevolent State passes a law against the sale of red ink. There was no law, however, to prevent *him* from drinking brandy, except the invincible law of his own intelligence, which he preferred to stifle for the moment. In spite of the warmth of the weather he felt cold. He ordered more brandy and a fire in his bedroom; he went up, sat down before it, and shivered.

Jacopo, whose eyes glistened at the sight of the fire, came up to him with letters. He stared at them blankly, and left them unopened.

"Will the Signore dine?"

"No, Jacopo, I am too busy."

He looked at his own empty, outstretched hands, and felt faintly amused. After the boy had gone he sat there a long time, staring stupidly into the fire. Then he drank some more brandy, which seemed to have no effect upon him, and began to stride up and down the room. He must write to her. His ideas were all blurred and misty in his head—he could not get them into focus. He sat down at the writing-table, and took up a pen. He wrote a few words, crossed them out, began again, tore the sheet, took another, and at the end of a quarter of an hour had written a whole sentence. Then suddenly he seemed to know what he wanted to say, and wrote steadily for a long time. This was what he said : —

LANGHAM HOTEL,
May 3.

"MY BELOVED—From my heart I thank you for the words you spoke to me to-day. What they were to me I cannot tell you. You love me. Whatever you choose, that is much—more than I deserve.

"Look, my darling. I can't say what is in my heart, what I write seems only words—words—words. I must trust to your sweet tenderness to read into them what I feel. I want to think of *you* first, but it's so hard.

"If you will marry me, child, I will give my life, every beat of it, every movement of my hands, every thought of my heart, to make you happier, and to restore.

"I know what I am saying, and I *will*. You love me. Can't you come to me? Can't you?

"If you *cannot,* I must not see you again. I know myself, and I know you. I *cannot* see you without having all of you, all to the last breath of your being. I know that would be your destruction and mine, it's not natural, it would make you hate me at the last. It can't be, it mustn't be. I could not go through again what I went through this afternoon, without bringing that destruction upon you and upon myself. There are limits—I know my own. If I once saw you again I couldn't stop myself. I should go with the tide and carry you with me. It mustn't be, I love you too much, but it is hard. I daren't stay within reach of you.

"If I do not have a word from you by 11 o'clock on Saturday morning, I leave for Singapore by the P. and O. steamship *Rangoon*. She touches at Malta, Brindisi, and Port Said. She will be at the last place on the 17th. In the enclosed paper are addresses which will find me. A word from you will bring me from the end of the world.

"My darling, have pity on me. You are so young, and the world is very big and beautiful, and time very merciful. Can't you come to me? If you love me, think of *yourself*, think of everything it must mean to *you*.

"Send me a word of hope! Tell me to wait. I love you so. The world is empty without you, the sun has no light, and there is no air. . . ."

The letter ended abruptly with those words. He made a fair copy of it, and read it through. While writing it he had had a certain feeling of satisfaction. He was at any rate doing something. But now, reading it, he thought "It is cold: It will never move her."

He sealed and addressed it, and as he did so he felt a great disgust with it and with himself. He stood with one foot on the grate holding it in his hand. The dying fire glowed with a sombre redness. He dropped the letter suddenly on the table with a groan, bent his forehead against the mantelpiece, and stared into the grate. Let it go! He could do no more. He looked at his watch, it was already ten o'clock. He felt very cold. There was still some brandy left and he drank it. With sudden energy he undressed, and got into bed. He thought, "I'll be done with it all; I'll get away to the East, there's always something going on there. Lots to see and do." He had a momentary glow in his heart; then he thought: "Without her! It's all empty!" And he turned his face to the wall.

.   .   .   .

The next morning he sent Jacopo with his letter, telling him to give it into Miss Ley's own hands, and knowing that he would be obeyed. The boy came back about noon.

"What did she say?" Giles asked.

"She thanked me, Signore."

"She gave you no message? Did she read the letter?"

The boy shook his head mournfully. From constant living with his master in lonely places he had an intuitive knowledge of the workings of his mind, and his own impressionable nature was wont to adapt itself accordingly.

"How did she look?"

"Her eyes were big and dark, Signore."

With that presentment of her he was obliged to be content. He sent Jacopo to take berths for Singapore, in the superstition, that if he prepared for the worst the best might come, the same feeling that makes a man take an umbrella out upon a fine day. No day that he had ever spent was quite as terrible as that day of waiting. He kept buying things for tropical use, telling himself that everything was settled, that she could not come, but he expected her all the time. The day dragged to its end.

She did not come.

On Saturday morning he drank brandy for breakfast—smoking was no use, but brandy was a good thing. The last year had been of use to him, he did not take trouble so resentfully. He was quiet under it, it seemed more a matter of course.

The brown was fading out of his face, he was hollow-eyed, and moved like a man recovering from an illness. He said to the hotel porter, a man who remembered him as a boy—

"If a lady calls for me or sends a message, a young lady with dark hair and eyes, *that* is the name, but perhaps she won't give a name," and he handed him a piece of paper with Jocelyn's name written on it—"Wire to me at Plymouth, Malta, Brindisi. I am going by the steamship *Rangoon,* there are written directions." He gave the man a ten-pound note. "It's important."

The man's countenance remained unmoved, but he was touched.

"I wish you luck, sir," he said; "you're not looking well, begging your pardon."

"Oh, I'm all right, thanks," said Giles with a smile.

A couple of hours later he went on board. That afternoon the *Rangoon* rounded the Foreland.

Chapter Twenty-six

In the reach of the Thames, just above Sonning Lock, a single sculling boat drifted slowly with the stream; though it was only the second week in May the river glowed with a soft radiance. The boat stole along under the left bank, over a chequered pattern of light and shade thrown on the water through the branches of the willow trees. Upon the far side of the river the hot sun laid a band of golden light spreading on to the path and over the green woods beyond. A slight breeze stirred with a gentle rustling, and a few fleecy clouds stood still in the blue sky.

Nielsen, in a white flannel suit, sat squarely on the rowing thwarts. Now and then he dipped his sculls in the water stiffly, from the elbows, with a motion somewhat suggestive of the "deep-sea" stroke. He had on white shoes and a broad white hat was pushed back from his forehead. His eyeglass was screwed into his eye, giving his face an expression of anxious concentration, ludicrously out of keeping with his attire and his occupation.

Jocelyn sat opposite him in the stern; the rudder lines were crossed idly in her lap, and she leant sideways, dangling a hand out of the boat and making little signs of the cross in the cool water. Sometimes she caught the young leaf of a water-lily plant, and then she would touch it softly with her fingers as if loth to let it go. She wore a blue skirt and a white silk blouse, which clung softly round the lines of her figure. Her jacket was thrown over the back of the seat, and a Japanese sunshade of a soft apricot colour lay unopened across her feet. She looked tired and languid;

on her face there was a grave pre-occupied look, and the corners of her mouth drooped a little.

Nielsen glanced over his shoulder. At the end of the long vista of rippling water and bending trees, the lock stretched, a black and sturdy line across the narrowing river. In the centre of it the figure of the lock-keeper could be seen leaning, in his shirt sleeves, over the railing of the foot-bridge.

"Shall we go through the lock?" said Nielsen.

Jocelyn looked up.

"I don't think there will be time," she said, "our train goes at half-past six. We passed a lovely backwater just now, let's go back to that and have tea."

Nielsen turned the boat round, and sculled slowly up-stream. He did not look quite at home in a boat, and he finished each stroke with a precision suggestive of earnest endeavour. It was too early in the year for river-folk, and with the exception of a fisherman's punt, their boat was the only one on the reach. Nielsen pulled through the entrance of the backwater, and ran the boat under a willow bank which formed a shelving islet in the centre. Jocelyn made tea. She handed Nielsen a cup, and he sat, very silent for him, alternately sipping it and puffing at a cigarette.

"What a heavenly day!" she said, with a sigh. Leaning back on the cushions of her seat, she glanced from side to side as if she would drink in to the full the calm beauty of the world. A little bird, sitting on an osier twig, cocked its head on one side, and chirped feebly—an answering chirp came from the branch above her head.

The rushes and the feathery grasses on the banks quivered as if the breeze were kissing them. A cuckoo called, another answered; two wood-pigeons flighted together across to the woods on the other side; a distant weir murmured gently, the willow branches over her head echoed it faintly, and the sun, breaking through the trees, made soft, white holes of light in the running water. A spirit of perfect harmony seemed to be looking gently at her from everywhere around. Her face clouded, and she made a quick movement with her hands. A startled water-rat dropped with a splash into the stream, and swam in a strenuous line for the other bank, where it scrambled to the mouth of its hole and sat calmly looking at her. Two swans with a brood of dusky infants paddled majestically past, hissing faintly; they disappeared up a

157

narrow passage of reed-grown water, leaving tiny eddies for a memory.

A furrow came between her brows. Nielsen, watching her, wondered. He sent a cloud of smoke through his lips.

"What is it you are thinking of?" he said at last. Jocelyn gave a little start, as if she had been brought back from very far.

"I was wondering," she said, "what it all means." She clasped her hands together, with their backs towards her. It was a motion that seemed to embrace all that was around them, and her eyes glanced at him with a troubled expression. The blue smoke from his cigarette was melting on all sides into the soft air.

"Even the smoke!" she said to herself quietly.

Nielsen did not answer—he did not understand. Jocelyn rested her chin in her hand; she was thinking: "Why isn't there a place for me to fill? Why am I always alone? Everything I see has a home, all the birds, and the trees, and the beasts, everything has its mate and its place. I am out in the cold—in the cold, always in the cold."

Nielsen was bending slightly forward on the seat, staring at her with his eyes screwed up. He held his cup in one hand and his cigarette in the other, and he seemed to have forgotten the existence of both.

There was a long silence, and the boat swayed once with some unseen stir of the water.

Jocelyn said suddenly—

"Do you believe in free will?"

Nielsen put down his cup, a little surprised at the sudden question, and threw away the end of his cigarette; it floated gently away from them, and stuck in some driftweed.

"Yes," he said, "and—no."

Jocelyn waited. He cleared his throat.

"That is a very difficult question, but I think it is like this, don't you know. One to another of us, has frree will; that is, you know, in our social relations. Looked at from the—er—the narrow point of view, there is of course frree will, yes—frree will, and we make use of it, as we are weak or strrong. But," and he spread his hands, and looking fixedly at the bank, "there is quite another point of view, don't you see, equally trrue; of course, we are all at the ends of long chains of—er—of circumstance. Whatever we do, you know, is only what comes out of that—it is all settled before, so that, of course, in that sense there is no frree will. For instance, my dear young lady, if you choose to do something unexpected, it is rreally the expected thing you are doing all the time, because the chains of your circumstances and your tempérrament would not permit you to do otherwise. I am afrraid I do not explain what I mean very well."

Jocelyn did not speak, she leaned forward with her chin on her hand gazing downwards.

Nielsen, with a puzzled look, rubbed his hands softly together. "Of course," he began again, "that is a verry brroad view, too brroad for everyday wear; it is—"

Jocelyn without looking up, interrupted him—

"And do you believe in morality?"

Nielsen sighed.

"Ah! What *is* morrality?"

He plucked a long blade of spikey grass from the bank, and said, twisting it in his fingers—

"What we *call* morrality—I believe in it," and he shrugged his shoulders. "Certainly. Why? Because *there* it is, don't you know? One can see it, it is quite thick, one can cut it with a knife. Every peoples has its own, and every peoples disobeys it more or less, don't you know; that is natural." He took out another cigarette, and began to nod his head up and down.

"Yes, yes," he said, continuing to nod his head. Presently he went on, fixing his eyes on the driftwood, where the end of the cigarette was giving up the ghost of its tobacco, and speaking to himself rather than to her. "Ah! it is a little thing, our morrality; but there is a big morrality , yes, yes, a *big* morrality, over there, don't you know," he pointed with his spike of grass towards the sweep of glistening water and the woods beyond.

"Over there!" he repeated, "everywhere! Yes, yes, Nature is verry morral. Ah! she is big, but she is morral. She *has* to be, you know. Look at that grass, my dear young lady," he said, holding up his spike of grass, and drawing it once or twice gently through his fingers, "she can't play frreaks, she has got her place, you know. It is wonderful to think, isn't it, if that little blade of grass vanished quite away, all the world would come undone. Ah! I think that is wonderful, *that* is morrality." He lit his cigarette and puffed at it thoughtfully.

"I think you know, everry man and woman has his place according to the big morrality—so have flies"—he went on, stabbing with his spike at an early fly which had settled on the rim of his cup—"and in spite of everrything they come to it at the last." He did not see Jocelyn's face. A wave of colour had rushed suddenly into it, and her eyes looked eager and startled; her lips moved—she was repeating to herself his words. A chance current swept the disembodied cigarette gently back past the boat, the paper and tobacco floated apart, pathetically close to each other.

"Ah!" said Nielsen, "there you are, my frriend; when we come apart like you, perrhaps we shall know all about it—this morrality." He straightened himself on his seat with a sudden jerk, and looking at Jocelyn remarked in an apologetic drawl—

"I am afrraid I have bored you drreadfully."

She was leaning back again on her cushions, twisting her fingers in her lap in the way peculiar to her when she was troubled or thinking deeply. Her face was still flushed, and her dark eye-lashes almost rested on her cheeks. A faint scent of May-blossom drifted to them from the bank. Nielsen threw away his cigarette. His eyes began to glow, his face suddenly lost its habitual apathy—the attitude of his mind was no longer leisurely. Indeed, it had not been leisurely for eight days, in fact, since he had passed Legard upon the stairs. Legard was gone, he had found that out, but he was still in a hurry.

His cheeks grew slightly red, a rare thing for him, and the lines deepened about his eyes. He bent forward as far as he could upon his seat, and the boat rocked slightly from side to side. He kept his eyes fixed upon her face. The colour was coming and going upon it. He fancied that her eyes were soft under their drooping lids, though he could not see them. Did she know that he was looking at her? Could she be thinking of him?

The long fingers were still twisting in and out of each other upon her knee. He put out his hand and touched one of them gently.

"I am waiting," he said; "I have been waiting so long."

She raised her eyes, and he was astonished at them. They were so large, and they changed as he looked at them. At first they were full of shrinking, almost of fear, then suddenly they blazed with excitement, which died away in a gentle look. She did not draw her hand away, she did not seem to know that he was touching her.

"I love you," he said. "Will you not marry me? I am always waiting."

It was curious that, generally so full of phrase and gesture, he was obliged to be quite simple in this matter. Her face did not change, but the corners of her mouth shaped themselves into a queer little smile. She did not speak at first, then she said softly—

"Wait a little longer," and her eyes seemed to be looking at something beyond him; "wait till to-morrow morning; I promise to tell you then—everything comes to its own place at the last, you know." His own words, but they sounded strange to him, as if used in some sense, he did not know what, which he had not intended for them. His face became puckered with the confusion of his thoughts. He bent it forward, and raising her hand, kissed it gently. She let him do it, but he was left with the feeling that she had known nothing of it.

Presently she rose suddenly to her feet, and stretched herself with a little shake, as if freeing herself from some weight. The colour rushed into her cheeks.

"Come," she said, "it's time to go."

Nielsen got out his sculls, and pushed out into the narrow stream. He said nothing more; with the kiss he had given her hand, he seemed to have relapsed into his usual patient resignation.

Every breath of wind had gone, the swallows were flying low, the hush of a perfect silence lay upon the river, yet there was felt rather than heard a mysterious singing, lost behind the veil of the blue sky—the voice of innumerable larks.

The sun, dropping into the west, laid a touch of warm light on Jocelyn's cheek when she turned and, looking behind her, as the boat shot through the narrow entrance, grasped at a drift of thistle-down floating aimlessly just out of her reach.

"That was like me," she said to herself softly.

Nielsen, occupied with his sculls, did not catch the words. All the way to Reading she was either moodily silent or talked with spasmodic gaiety. She kept saying nervously, "You don't think we shall lose the train, do you?"

As they were walking to the station from the river, she suddenly stood still, and said to Nielsen—

"D'you remember that picture we saw at Watts's studio—the 'Paolo'?"

"Yes," he answered, "a dreadful picture."

"It was *not* dreadful," she said, "it was beautiful—you don't see the meaning in it. I didn't then, but I do now. There was 'union' in that picture—'union' in spite of everything else. I never realised it before."

Before he could answer, she started to walk again. He did not understand her.

It was nearly half-past eight before they got to the Mansions. Jocelyn asked him to come in and have some supper, but she did not appear herself, sending a message from her room to say that she was very tired, and was going straight to bed. Mrs. Travis accepted the excuse with a wry face—she disliked the trouble of entertaining single-handed; she made no remonstrance, however. During the last few days, she had found Jocelyn so variable in her moods, so silent and restless, that for the sake of comfort she mildly accepted any conduct at her hands. It had so happened that she had heard nothing of Legard's reappearance, but she had been acutely conscious of something disturbing, for which she neither knew, nor cared to know, the reason. She never dived below the surface.

Nielsen took his departure early. The paramount impression on his mind as he drove back to his hotel was that of uneasy perplexity; it did not, however, prevent him from sleeping soundly.

The next morning he rose early, and dressed very carefully. He made a good breakfast, eating it slowly and earnestly, as if he wished to place each morsel where it would be of the greatest service to him. During breakfast he entered into conversation, over the top of his newspaper, with an old gentleman at the adjoining table, to whom he gave much useful advice as to the treatment of lumbago. He had never had it himself. When he had finished his paper, he went out.

It was a beautiful morning, and he moved leisurely along with his square walk, turning every now and then to look at somebody, generally a lady, and removing his grey top-hat politely if he chanced to brush against any one in the crowded street. He stopped at his hairdresser's, and went in. He had his hair cut, discussing affably with the man the political situation, and a new instrument for crimping hair. When he came out again he drew his gloves on to his round, freckled hands, and hailed a hansom. He directed the man to "Wills & Segar's," where he bought a beautiful bouquet of roses and lilies, and an orchid for his own buttonhole. He lectured the florist for two minutes upon the injustice of demanding eighteenpence for his orchid, and gave half-a-crown to a ragged child he found on the doorstep. He told the cabman to drive him to the Mansions. As the cab bowled down to the Embankment, his pale, broad face under its white hat looked out over the bouquet with the weary, anxious expression of a dog sitting on its hind legs.

Arrived at the Mansions, he went up the stairs slowly, holding his bouquet carefully in front of him, and stopping at the top to wipe his forehead. He felt very nervous. The maid, who let him in, looked scared and troubled, and he detained her a moment in the passage to inquire after her health. He was such a constant visitor that he was admitted to the drawing-room without special announcement.

He placed his bouquet upon the table, and rubbed his hands together. A door opened behind him, and Mrs. Travis came into the room. She was incongruously majestic in black silk and a rose-coloured bonnet with humming-birds in it. She did not shake hands, but held a note out to him. Nielsen looked at her face as he took it. It gave him the impression that she had somehow neglected to finish it that morning. It was, so to speak, patchy, and there were strange and sudden wrinkles round her mouth and eyes. This was alarming to him, as no words could have been. He bowed over her hand, and opened his note.

Mrs. Travis said nothing, but stood in front of him, puffing her lips. His note was from Jocelyn, and it was in these words:—

"DEAR MR. NIELSEN,—What you wish of me *can never be*. You don't know me, or what I am. If you did, you would not ask me. I am going away—'to my own place.' I am very, *very* sorry if I hurt you, you are so good, and so kind. Will you be like yourself, and take care of my aunt a little? I'm afraid she will miss me at first.—Yours ever sincerely,

"JOCELYN LEY."

He read it over a second time. "To my own place." What did she mean? The words were familiar. Ah! Yes! his own words. He did not understand, but he was dimly conscious that in some way he had ministered to his own defeat. He looked up, and encountered Mrs. Travis's green eyes.

"She is gone!" he said slowly, and as if he wanted to impress the fact upon his own mind.

"Yes, she is gone!" he repeated, and looked at Mrs. Travis's face. It was twitching nervously, and her eyes were not still for a moment.

"Where?" he said abruptly, and sat stiffly down in a chair. Mrs. Travis's hand sought her pocket.

"I don't know," she said at last, taking out a letter and her handkerchief, "I have had this—a dreadful letter. She says she will write, and that we are not to fuss about her—to fuss," she sniffed, and went on—

"I came down late to breakfast, and the servant told me she had gone, the naughty girl, and taken her maid and her boxes and dressing-bag, and left me this note. I don't know what to do—she has her own money. Of course I can't do anything. It's not right. What will people say, what will people think?"

Nielsen heard, but he did not answer, he was thinking of other things, and he sat staring at his bouquet with little puckers at the corners of his brown eyes. He drummed with the fingers of one hand upon his knee. The note had fallen out of them, and Jocelyn's kitten, straying from a corner, patted it furtively with a grey paw. His reverie was painful, and yet it was tinted with a characteristic philosophy. Perhaps it did not hurt him quite so much as he thought. She was lost to him! How beautiful she had been! It was curious, but true, that he already thought of her in the past tense. He smoothed his moustache. Yes! It hurt! The kitten clawed his trousers, and climbed up on to his knee.

"Poor little cat!" he muttered. He felt sorry for the cat. It had a forlorn little face, and it mewed, probably because his trousers were slippery, and because he had no lap.

"Poor little cat!" This was going to be a serious business for them both, eh? He dangled the end of his eyeglass in front of its nose. The kitten cheered up somewhat, and bit it. Nielsen watched it with sympathy. A bad business! He wrinkled his nose thoughtfully, and his face looked older.

A sigh from the other end of the room attracted his attention. It came from Mrs. Travis. She was sitting, tremblingly upright, upon the sofa, constantly smoothing, with a large white hand, the note in her lap. Her face seemed to have become suddenly flabby like a pudding; her cheeks had lost much of their colour; one long end of her fringe dangled into her left eye, and she puffed her lips incessantly. She said nothing; her pride did not allow her to utter any word of complaint, but her green eyes were alive with resentment. The bottom had fallen out of the chair of her comfort, and left her—a large child, pathetic and ridiculous—sitting upon air.

Nielsen put the kitten gently on the floor and got up. He walked across the room, sat squarely down upon the sofa, and took her hand in his.

Chapter Twenty-seven

AT Port Said the *Rangoon* was coaling. Legions of black and brown men swarmed at her from the unkempt rafts alongside. Half naked, gleaming with perspiration, chattering and laughing, they poured into her an unending stream of coal.

The passengers were escaping into the town, besieged by a motley set of rascals, masterpieces of ugliness and iniquity, with cries of "Hi, hi, Master—Tararaboomdeay—Mrs. Langtry—Hi —Charlie—Porter, sah?—Very good guide, dis fella, Master." Nobody wanted them, nobody engaged them, but they followed yelping like a pack of curs.

Legard, walking rapidly through the streets, inquiring his way here and there, went straight to the post-office. He had received nothing at other places, but it was a formality which he continued to observe. There was nothing. He came out again, and stood in the street, biting his lips, with a sick, leaden sensation of defeat, and mechanically began to calculate the next possible place at which he might have news. He stared about him blankly. In the sprawling, ill-kept streets the hot wind, creeping unexpectedly round corners, raised little eddies of sand, and crept away again, leaving them stagnant. Jews, Greeks, Turks, infidels and heretics, lounged and loafed outside the shops, in every variety of costume; now and then, threading stolidly between them, parties of his fellow-passengers passed, their faces for the most part expressive of a continual exclamation, smothered in a continual sniff. He began to walk about, wandering idly into shops, exchanging a nod here and there with some ship acquaintance. His thoughts were bitter, and yet his attention was half distracted from them by the strange chatter and movement around him.

The sea had done him good, he no longer looked ill, only very fine-drawn. On the second day of the voyage he had given up brandy; he used to tramp about the deck by himself, or stand in the bows with Shikari, looking at the water hissing up the ship's side.

His thoughts ran perpetually in one channel. If she wished it to be an episode, let it be; he would tear her image out of his heart, drop the past year out of his life, as if it had never been; and then—he would suddenly have a sense of degradation, a feeling as if his heart were shrinking within him, like a plant closing its leaves at the touch of something rough and foreign to it; the old pain and longing would begin again, and he would think of her as a tender, helpless child to whom he *must* be good, at all costs to himself—yes! to whose memory even he must be good. He sometimes wished the thing would break him up, and let him go comfortably to the dogs, and he felt exasperation because he somehow knew it would not.

He remained gently unapproachable to people on board, but he made friends with some children, one of whom, a dark-eyed, brown-faced child, reminded him in a mysterious way of Jocelyn. She was not in the least like her, except that she had the same tiny dimples at the corners of her mouth when she smiled. She left the ship, however, at Brindisi, and he gave her his watch, to which she had taken a fancy.

He had always loved the sea, and now she served him; her many moods gave him something outside himself to think about. The days seemed very long, but all the time, without knowing it, he got stronger and calmer. The great sea is a wonderful soother of sorrowing. For the time that she takes a man into her keeping, he is not torn, but rather rocked by sorrow, with a gentle heaving as of many waters. She brings not forgetfulness, but sympathy. So Giles found. . . .

When he had strolled aimlessly about the streets for some time, he went into an hotel, and, sitting down, waited till it should please an unwilling providence to give him lunch. Many of his fellow-passengers were in the room, the waiters ran distractedly here and there, and nothing seemed to result. That is a peculiarity of Port Said when ships are in.

Two men sitting at a table near him, but hidden by a column, began to talk.

"Beastly hole!" said the first.

He recognised the voice for that of a man of about his own age, who had lost one of his legs, and wore a wooden one.

"When I was coming out lást year with my friend, Lord Cardrew," said the other man, "we—er—hadn't even time to go up the—er—water tower. Such a beautiful view from it; you must come with me and see it."

The speaker was an old fellow of sixty, travelling for his health; a man with a tanned face, clean-shaven, but for the white moustache running in a straight close-clipped line above a lip which displayed his rather yellow upper teeth. A retired diplomat, a dilettante in art, tall, dapper, a stickler for ceremony and the aristocracy, of which he was not a member, he habitually wore a yachting cap, and pronounced the word ghastly—gástly.

Giles had heard his private history, and knew him for a man who had suffered much at the hands of his wife and children, and who lived perpetually in the fear of death from a bad heart.

"*À propos* of my friend, Lord Cardrew, there is a man on board very like him; his name is—er—Legard. I wonder if he is one of the—Legards. I would ask him, but he—er—never seems to speak to anybody."

The other voice said—

"Tall, rather dark chap, I know—seems very down in the mouth —here, waiter, bring some ice."

Giles shifted uneasily in his seat.

The old fellow went on—

"Poor fellow—nice-looking fellow he is too—a woman, I suppose."

Giles rose softly from his seat and went out of the room. He experienced a sudden feeling of shame, of disgust with himself. He told himself bitterly that he had no monopoly of trouble, that he should make himself a stock for the chatter of any casual bystander. Either of these two men, who had been talking, had more claim to compassion than himself.

He strode on angrily, till, on the outskirts of the town, a desolate expanse of sand and of brackish water confronted him in cheerless immensity. He stood there for a long time, while the hot wind swept past him.

A sense of his own insignificance was upon him. What did his emotions matter? What was he? A tiny fragment in the eternal scheme, which the scorching wind of life had dried and passed by, a fragment as hard, as unmingled, and as lonely as the grains of sand which he rubbed between his hands. After all, was he not himself a single grain in a wilderness of bitter sand?

Life was a weary business; he had made a mess of his, and nothing mattered much now! He hated himself for his lack of pluck. He turned on his heel presently, and went back through the town, and got on board.

A gentle grime was over everything, and they were cleaning down. He shut himself up in his cabin, and lay on his bunk trying to read. Two hours later the *Rangoon* got up steam and entered the canal.

He went in to dinner as usual. After all, there is a law that a man must eat, and another law that his emotions shall not stand still, but shift always back and forwards. He made spasmodic efforts to talk during dinner, but he felt both dull and reckless, and they were not a success.

When he went up, the decks were cleared for dancing, an awning was spread over them. Chinese lanterns swayed gently from poles, and, here and there, seats were placed cunningly in dark corners.

The ship glided smoothly along the narrow belt of water, with a slight list to port.

Giles, leaning over the rail, smoked, and watched the light of the summer evening slowly give way, and sink into the distant sand mountains of the West.

The band came up and began to play a waltz, and people moved uneasily about the decks, like ducks before they take the water. The ship's lamps shone feebly through the twilight, and stars began to creep up into the receding heavens. He walked forward and stood in the round of the promenade deck, looking towards the bows. The darkness gathered; in front the tail light of a steamer glowed like a fiery eye; the canal banks, and here and there the outline of buildings or of fencing, showed in sharp, black lines through the clear dusk. Over his shoulder he could see the lanterns swinging, lonely discs of coloured lights, and catch the gleam of white skirts. Laughter and voices, music, and the hushed hoot of the steam-whistle sprang into the still night.

169

Sometimes in a lull of the dancing, when nothing sounded but the dumb beat of the screw, the desert wind stole softly past, and whispered in the awning over his head. The magic of the night wrapt him, and he thought—

"There must be something in it all. I am on the wrong tack," and again the whisper of the wind, and the faint cry of flighting quails, would come to him through the darkness, seeming to speak of something hidden, of something behind the veil, which may perhaps be reached through pain and work and much self-sacrifice, some secret, great and universal.

"Yes," he thought, watching the smoke of his cigar curl away, "I am on the wrong tack."

He thought of his life, the emptiness and waste of it. What had he ever done for anybody? Nothing. Nothing, except bring harm. He thought of his mother and his school-days, of what she had thought he would become—of all the unbroken waste of his life since. What had he done? How had he gained the right to live in a world where all things must move forward or die? The music started again, there was a light laugh, and, as he stood back in the shadow, a man and a girl passed him leaning towards each other. The deck quivered under his feet with the beat of the screw. Something stirred in him, something strenuous. He thought, "Is it too late? is there *nothing* in me? *nothing* for me to do?"

The man and the girl passed again, he was whispering to her, and she twisted a flower in her hands. Memory came to Giles with the scent from it. He shrank back. "Without her! O God!" he thought, and pulled his cap over his eyes.

He sat there long. The dancing ceased, but people stayed on deck, waiting for the ship to reach Ismailia. The moon had risen, and the lamps hung colourless in the white glory of her light. The ship seemed to glide on a band of silver between rolling steppes of snow, but always the wind was the breath of the fiery desert. On the main deck below he could see steerage passengers sleeping uneasily, tossing from side to side with shirts open at the neck, patches of grey on the white of the burnished ship. He looked at his watch. It was twelve o'clock. The ship idled along, slowing down now and then with a faint hissing sound, as the white steam escaped from her sides into the whiter air. With a feeling of wary impatience he resented the dragging motion—it was like his life, where nothing ever happened—a desolate and an empty waste of time.

He had a longing to get out of it, to get to the end, to find something to do—something incessant and exhausting, which day by day would dull his feeling in sheer weariness. Presently he fell back again into his chair in the shadow of the hurricane deck above, and dozed off into an uneasy sleep. Through it he felt all the time the silent plains of snow-white sand, the dim flash of lights, the jar of the screw, the hiss of steam, and the striking of the ship's bell, mingled in a misty confusion with strange words and shapes, the fantastic creatures of his dreams. He woke up when the ship stopped at Ismailia, heard the hurrying of feet, the cry of voices giving orders, the prolonged blast of the whistle; then the jar of the screw began once more under his feet, and he dozed again.

Chapter Twenty-eight

HE woke from restless and bitter dreams, feeling stiff and a little cold. The moon was sinking in the sky, and only patches of white light fell now upon the decks. He raised himself in his chair to look about him. A woman was leaning against the port bulwark looking out over the desert. As his eyes fell upon her figure he moved uneasily, and a shiver passed through his limbs. She turned, and began to walk towards him into the darkness of the shadow. His eyes rested on her face—and he gasped. He thought "I am dreaming."

She seemed like a tender vision of slumber and of memory, stepping to him out of the night. He rubbed his eyes, and got up very gently from his chair. She stopped, and he could see her lips quiver, she was so close to him. He held out his hands silently— he was afraid that at some word of his she would vanish, as she had come, into the night. She took one step, and touched him—her lips parted.

"I have come, you see," she said, and she leaned against him. His arms were round her, his face was buried in her hair, but no word passed his lips.

'I've come to do what you wish, after all. I couldn't help it— something there"—and she touched her chest with her hand— "there wasn't any other place for me, you see."

She spoke like a tired child, and rubbed her cheek softly against his shoulder. Then suddenly she raised her face, tender and mysterious in the gloom, and kissed him on the lips. Tears ran silently down his face, and she kissed them. She raised her arms, drew his head down to her breast, and held it there. And, while they stood, the hot wind soughed faintly above them; once, the bell rang out two sharp strokes, the cry of the watchman fled weirdly into the night, and the ship slept again to the hum of her screw and the bubble of the silver water. And now great shadows stalked along the cold sands, like the uneasy thoughts of a dream; and sometimes a feeble cry would speak to them out of the heart of the desert.

Giles raised his head at last, and holding her fast in his arms whispered, "Tell me!"

"I belong to you. I knew it when you were gone. I belonged to you ever since—that night." Her cheek was hot against his own, and he could feel the beating of her heart. "I will be your wife, darling; I will do anything you tell me, I won't ever hurt you again."

He could only say, " 'Sh!" and stroke her face gently with his hand. He looked at it under its little, soft grey cap, as it rested against his shoulder. Her eyes glanced up at him, large, and full of living light, and then drooped like a sleepy child's under their heavy lids. He was dumb with the passion of tenderness which filled him for the frail girl, who had come to him from so far. How marvellously sweet to him was every tiny trembling of her slender body, every breath that came through her parted lips! How dear, every whisper of her voice!

He said in a husky voice: "How did you come, my little one?"

She rested a hand on this chest, and pulled at the button of his coat.

"I was afraid I shouldn't catch you, they told me to come from Marseilles. I was very lucky, there was a boat, and I came to Alexandria and Cairo. When I got to Ismailia, I was just in time; I told my maid to ask if you were on board, and then I came, and I'm *so* tired."

She dropped her head on his shoulder again with a little sigh.

"I have come," she said, "and oh! *I love you so.*"

His face quivered with a throbbing tenderness that was like pain. With each beat of his heart the muffled footfall of the watch officer sounded across and across the deck above; and, ghostly in the slanting light of the moon, some dhows glided past in the tow of a tiny, puffing launch. His arms closed round her till her heart beat against him; and a great shudder of passion ran through his frame.

"By all the life in me, child," he said huskily, "I will make up to you for the past—we will wipe it out together."

She looked up at him, and for a moment her eyes seemed to brim over with the tenderness in them, then they gazed at him, suddenly dark and profound, out of a sad little face. A tiny wisp of her hair fell loose across her ear.

"Yes—if we can." Her voice, hushed and uncertain, was like a prayer to Fate, but her hand touched his cheek with soft fingers. 'Who knows?"

The wind carried the whisper away into the remoteness of the desert.

THE END